I0608473

SEX ON THE SEATS

LOVE AFTER MIDNIGHT #4

ELISE FABER FABER

SEX ON THE SEATS
BY ELISE FABER

This is a work of fiction. Names, places, characters, and events are fictitious in
every regard. Any similarities to actual events and persons, living or dead, are
purely coincidental. Any trademarks, service marks, product names, or named
features are assumed to be the property of their respective owners and are used
only for reference. There is no implied endorsement if any of these terms are
used. Except for review purposes, the reproduction of this book in whole or part,
electronically or mechanically, constitutes a copyright violation.

SEX ON THE SEATS
Copyright © 2021 Elise Faber
Print ISBN-13: 978-1-946140-93-7
Ebook ISBN-13: 978-1-946140-94-4
Cover Art by Jena Brignola

LOVE AFTER MIDNIGHT

Rum And Notes

Virgin Daiquiri

On The Rocks

Sex On The Seats

CHAPTER ONE

Dominique

I DIDN'T KNOW what in the fuck I was doing in a bar at midnight on a weeknight.

Not sleeping.

Not getting drunk.

Not working.

Not doing anything aside from nursing the single beer that Hayden's girlfriend had pulled for me several hours ago.

And staring at myself in the mirror behind the bar, wondering how in the world I'd gotten to this place.

Less in an at-the-actual-bar question and more of a what-the-fuck-was-I-doing-with-my-life sort of way. I'd built connections in the world of private military operations. I took down bad guys on the regular with hardly more than my computer and my wits.

But . . . I didn't have that.

That being what the rest of this fucking bar composed almost entirely of couples had.

Love.

Multiple different groups of couples in the booths in the

back, all with affection shining in their eyes while they partook in nonstop cuddling. It was sickening . . . and something I'd witnessed many times over in the last hours since Hayden had dragged me here after one of our few in-person meetings.

We'd needed to devise a strategy to take down a ring of hackers trying to sell people's personal information, a really fucking sneaky ring, and sometimes that meant having to look outside the box . . . or the secure chat window that was my preferred mode of contact.

Look, I *could* schmooze and be charming and woo new clients just as easily as I could hack through someone's firewall.

But two guesses as to which I preferred.

And it really better only take one.

Anyway, I knew I should have left hours before, but something had made me stay. Maybe the handsome black bartender, who'd swept his beautiful blond girlfriend up into a kiss when she'd brought him a plate of cookies—and yes, I was good enough at my job to know that the bartender was Brent and his fiancé was Iris. I'd done a full background on Hayden before I hired him, including his sister and her boyfriend, Kace, who owned the bar. *All* of whom were currently spending the majority of their time mooning over their significant others. Hayden to the pretty and spunky Anabelle, who I quite liked and seemed to alternate between faux annoyance with Hayden and love shining in those deep brown eyes. Since annoyance was an emotion I readily identified with, I could at least support *that* type of mooning. On the other hand, Kace and Brooke were nauseating.

Brooke was too damned cute with her pencil behind one ear, her red hair askew, her eyes focused on her laptop even as she and Kace seemed to unconsciously orbit one another.

When he was near, she shifted unconsciously in her seat, though her fingers didn't stop. And he didn't interrupt, just pressed a kiss to the top of her head, brushing his knuckles over her cheek, her nape, her arm, filling the glass in front of her with soda at regular intervals.

Love. Caring for one another. Instinctive.

Fucking fairy tales under neon bar signs.

"Here," a silken male voice said.

Ignoring the way that voice slid over my skin, as though he were running a piece of delicate silk over my naked body, I glanced up into a pair of stunning hazel eyes. The different shades of green and gold and brown mixed together in a way that was both beautiful and completely unique.

But I didn't react on the outside.

First, I'd seen plenty of beautiful men in my life. Second, I'd felt him approach, but since he'd spent the vast majority of the night well away from me, I hadn't bothered to look too closely.

Not a threat. Moving on.

Now, I glanced down to see the drink in front of me. An orange and red concoction with a cherry floating on top of some ice cubes. A cheery red straw was perched on the side.

"What's this?" I asked.

He rolled those gorgeous, unique eyes, and I actually felt my skin prickle in awareness. "Sex on the Beach."

"Excuse me?" It was an arched question that sent amusement tap-dancing through his expression.

"Their"—he nodded at a group of couples hovering near his end of the bar—"ladies' night was apparently crashed by their husbands. Now they're enjoying ordering the dirtiest cocktails they can think of and having the men pay the tab. I mixed one too many and figured you could use something that wasn't warm beer."

I ran my finger through the condensation on the outside of the glass. "And Sex on the Beach was the dirtiest they could think of?"

"Apparently." Lips twitching, he nudged it closer. "Have a sip. Despite the cheesy name, it's actually pretty good." He nodded at my beer. "And since you don't seem to be enjoying your beer . . ."

"I'm not much of a beer girl."

"What kind of girl are you?"

Uh-oh.

The way he said that, with the quiet note of heat hidden beneath all that silk, was troublesome. Even more troublesome was my body's reaction.

Moisture pooled between my thighs. My nipples went tingly.

Nope. Not gonna do it.

I lifted my chin. "First of all, I'm a woman, not a girl."

Hazel eyes dipped down before returning to mine, a slow smile curving his mouth. That smile was . . .

Fucking hell.

I shifted on my barstool, thighs clenching together because . . . that smile was pure, unadulterated sex.

On the seats.

An image of him spreading my legs, of those broad shoulders pushing my thighs wide as he pressed those lush lips to my pussy made the alarm bells transform into hurricane sirens.

Because I was imagining having sex on the seats.

With a stranger.

With a stranger I wanted more than I wanted my careful distance.

Oh. *Shit.*

CHAPTER TWO

Dominique

"WHAT'S YOUR NAME?" I asked quietly.

"Archer."

I sniffed. "That's a ridiculous name."

He shrugged. "Maybe." A nudge of the glass toward me. "You going to try it?"

"Is it drugged?"

He grinned. "You'll never know till you try it," he drawled.

Sighing, trying to stifle the desire drawing me to this stranger, I put the straw to my lips and sucked.

His eyes went hot.

I almost came on that seat.

And then the sweet and tart drink hit my tongue.

"You like it," he said, voice husky.

I pushed the glass away. "No."

"You do."

"It's too sweet," I protested.

His hand covered mine. "Like you."

I slipped my fingers free, leaned back in the seat. "And you're out of your fucking mind."

Those hazel eyes sparkled under the lights overhead, and fuck, every time I looked at them, I got lost in them. They were so changeable and intoxicating, unlike anything I'd ever laid *eyes* on . . . pun intended.

"Maybe it would be more truthful for me to say, I bet *you'd* taste sweet?"

More thigh-clenching.

More moisture gathering.

More uncomfortable shifting on my seat.

"What about you?" I asked, my voice husky with need. Not that I could do a damned thing about eliminating that rasp. I wanted him, and it had been a long time. Ages, even. I'd been too busy building my work, my life, my strength, my . . . power.

I hadn't spared any brainpower to do anything but work.

But now my work didn't require as much energy; the business ran on its own more often than not. So, aside from the occasional meeting like I'd needed to conduct tonight with Hayden, I had found myself with time of late.

And if there was something that I didn't like having copious amounts of, it was free time.

Even before work had taken over my life the last few years, I had always been one of those people who never failed to have something going—a place to visit, something to do around my house. Hell, I'd even done my fair share of crafts. It would probably surprise the hell out of the people I let glimpse slivers of my life, but I could quilt, crochet, and cross-stitch with the best of them.

But my favorite thing was computers—hacking into systems that were designed to keep people like me out, finding the shit that bad guys wanted to keep hidden.

And then turning it over to my clients . . . or the appropriate authorities.

Either one.

Depending on what was found.

Depending on what *I* chose.

That was written into my ironclad NDA, my approved-by-multiple-lawyers contract.

"Do *I* taste sweet?" Archer replied, pulling me out of my head and back into the conversation that was prickling with sexual awareness, sending waves of tingling sensations over my nape, my stomach . . . lower. "Is that what you're asking?"

I took a sip of the drink, enjoying the concoction despite myself. "A pretty boy like you? You're saccharine." I sniffed. "You're *sickly* sweet."

He plunked his elbows on the bar, leaned forward. "Is that so?"

My eyes dipped, catching on his hands. Big hands, a few scars crossing their backs, hair sprinkled up his muscular forearms.

Strong arms were kryptonite.

Mine.

I could image them banding around me, picking me up and hauling me close, setting me on this very bar top as he stepped between my thighs. I could almost feel their hardness against me, a phantom touch stroking my skin, fueling my rising need.

"Yes," I murmured. "That's *exactly* so."

"Mmm."

He patted the bar, sending that image blazing to full color, then straightened and returned to the other end of the bar, and I spent the next ten minutes pretending I didn't notice him while I finished the drink.

That I definitely didn't notice his ass, glorious and plump, or his thighs straining at the denim encasing his legs. Certainly, I didn't notice that his biceps stretched the sleeves of his shirt or that he had a tattoo on his back, creeping up and out of the neck of that tight black cotton, caressing his skin in a pattern I was desperate to trace with my tongue.

I didn't notice any of that.

Nor that I'd reached the bottom of my glass.

Until he turned to face me, his eyes flicking toward my hands.

My own gaze dropped, and I took in the ice, the dredges of juice and alcohol. Then my eyes lifted, drifted to those forearms, those thighs, that *ass*.

And alarm bells continued to blare.

I watched him lean close to Kace, whisper in his ear.

Kace nodded, but I didn't bother to stick around any longer. The blaring of all the warning signals had grown too loud. They were deafening, thrumming through me in a rhythm that urged me to go. I reached into my purse, threw thirty bucks on the counter—drinks in the Bay Area were expensive—then pushed off my stool.

I needed sex.

I *wanted* it with the man on the other end of the bar, with *Archer*.

I stood by my reasoning that it was a stupid name.

Gorgeous, sexy man. Terrible, *terrible* name.

Sighing, I slipped my small wallet into the front pocket of my jeans—jeans I'd had specially tailored because clothing manufacturers had decided somewhere along the line that women didn't need pockets that actually fit useful things like wallets or phones. Oh no, we only needed room for our lipstick, for some mascara, maybe a breath mint so that we could blow dudes with minty freshness.

Fun times.

Deliberately keeping my eyes away from Terrible Name, I wove through the crowd, thinner now than it had been hours before, then slipped into the hall.

The back room where I'd hung with Hayden was quieter than the large space in the front of the building. The bigger area was wall-to-wall with people much younger than me, the music newer, the furnishings sleek metal and glass and stone compared to the warm wood of the back, slightly sticky from use.

I was clearly the wrong age for the trendy front space and the right for the comfort and nostalgia the back space brought to mind.

On the heels of that thought, a man—or really, a *boy*—stepped in front of me, blocking my path. He was handsome but young, way too young and cocky to tempt me. Like a frat boy who'd just aged out of his fraternity but still thought for some reason that every woman would fawn over him like they were freshmen and he was a sexy senior.

Skeeved. Me. As in, this man-child skeeved me out.

"Hi, baby," he said, his gaze dipping down and back up.

A tendril of disgust wound through me, coiling in my stomach, sliding up my spine, obliterating the desire for Archer that had left my panties damp.

"Not interested," I said, pushing past him.

"Hey, wait—"

He grabbed my arm.

I froze, glanced down at his hand on me, unwelcome and uninvited. My brows rose as I met his stare. "What do you think you're doing?"

His fingers tightened. "I'm trying to talk to you."

"And *I said*, I'm not interested," I gritted. "Take your hand off me."

But he left it in place, had the balls to draw me a little closer, until I could smell the fermented yeast on his breath, until it felt as though I were drinking another beer just from the scent of his exhales . . . and maybe it was exuding its odor through his pores.

Lovely.

"Baby, I just want to talk to you." He drew me a little closer still.

I sighed, reached for his hand, gripping between thumb and forefinger, digging my nails into the pressure point there. I wasn't gentle in the least, and his fingers spasmed, his hand opened, releasing my arm. "You don't get to touch me."

He yanked his hand out of my grip. "Bitch. I can do what I want."

"No." I glared up at him. "Asshole." I held his gaze. "You don't have permission to touch me. *Ever.* So back the fuck—"

One second, he was there in front of me, his blue eyes glittering with malice, his lips pressed into a flat line, and the next, he was pinned against the wall behind me, Archer's elbow shoved against his throat. "You don't *fucking* touch her."

A huge man, bald as a newborn and with bulky shoulders, appeared at Archer's back. "Problem?" he asked calmly.

"This handsy motherfucker needs to go."

"My friends—" Frat Boy began.

"Can join your ass on the curb," the bouncer said, gripping his arm, and not gently by the way Frat Boy winced, his skin going pale. His volume lifted over the din of noise. "Who's with this asshole?"

The crowd went quiet, wide eyes connecting over heads until finally a few hands lifted.

"With me," the bouncer said.

"Thanks, Eli," Archer said.

A nod before he shifted his eyes to me, the giant's eyes gentle. "Sorry I missed him."

My lips parted, a breath escaping. Because I felt oddly touched by the mountain of a man's regret. "It's okay," I said.

"Not okay." Another nod, and then Eli was growling to Frat Boy, "If you ever want to show your face in any bar in this area again, you will apologize, get the fuck out, and learn how to keep your fucking hands to yourself."

"Look how she's dressed," Frat Boy spat. "Bitch is practically on display—"

I lifted my chin, crossed my arms, and shot daggers at him through my eyes. "Are you fucking serious right now? You're coming at me with the clothes I'm wearing? Did I fall asleep and end up in 1954?" Oh, if only I had a superpower, *any* superpower. I would pay for said superpower in the blood of . . .

earthworms? (Did they have blood?) Anywho, I digressed, because the point was that I would cheerfully murder the asshole man-child right at the moment.

Eli twisted Frat Boy's arm behind his back, started to frog-march him away. "And congrats, you've now earned yourself a spot on the Pub List. Good luck getting a drink in the surrounding thirty miles."

"Fuck you."

"Ah." Eli smiled. "I knew that you were special." He leaned close. "Let's make it fifty miles."

With that, Frat Boy and Eli walked out of the bar, his friends following him. The moment the exterior door closed, the noise picked up inside, conversations resuming, eyes leaving me as gazes returned to their own parties.

"You okay?" Archer asked.

I spun to face him. "I had him."

Hazel eyes sparkled. "I know." One half of his mouth curved, ticking up, and I felt that smirk all the way to my pussy.

Fuck.

I spun away from him, heading for the door, my mind on my vibrator, knowing that Happy Time would be accompanied with a side of bearded, hazel-eyed Archer with the powerful thighs and sexy smile.

It wasn't until I pushed outside, turned in the direction of my car that I realized the prickling between my shoulder blades wasn't the man's gaze on me, but rather, because Archer was following me. "What the hell do you think you're doing?" I gritted, my voice quiet because the air outside the bar was muted, the vast majority of the noise contained by the building and its thick walls, and I knew he could hear me.

"Walking you to your car."

Said so matter-of-factly that I nearly stumbled.

As though I were an idiot for not understanding what he was doing, as though it were common for men to come to my rescue.

Well, it *wasn't* common, thank me very much.

I didn't need rescue.

I saved myself.

"Why?" I asked as I turned the corner, spotted my car up ahead, knowing it didn't matter, that I shouldn't be doing anything to prolong the conversation, that I should relegate this man to fantasies and special time spent with my vibrator.

He moved so he walked abreast of me.

And seriously, but thinking about breasts didn't help the situation. Not when mine felt so heavy, my nipples tingling. I could practically feel his rough hands on my skin. When he'd touched me earlier, reaching across the dark blond wood of the bar, his palm had been calloused, demonstrating no shortage of hard work. He wasn't a Frat Boy or a man who spent all his time pecking at a keyboard—

Not that I had a problem with that, since *I* spent most of my time pecking at my keyboard.

But I liked my men to be . . . *men.*

More danger and alarm bells and tsunami sirens.

"Shouldn't you be back behind that bar, slinging drinks?" I asked, maybe a bit desperately.

"Nope."

I tilted my gaze up, met his eyes. They looked dark brown in the moonlight, glimmers of silver in their depths. "Nope?"

"Nope," he repeated.

Seriously?

I bit back a sigh, continued walking, determined to finally ignore him, as I should have done from the moment my ass had hit the seat back in the bar. And I succeeded. Sort of. Because even though I bit back my inquiry demanding that he tell me why he shouldn't be doing his damned job, I was still curious. Heaven help me.

"I got off shift three hours ago," he said when I was just about to burst.

This time, I *did* stumble.

And warm fingers caught my arm, steadied me.

"Not going to ask me why I stayed on?" he asked, a hint of amusement in his tone, like he knew it was killing me to not pump him for information.

But also . . . no. I wasn't going to ask him.

Because I knew.

It was the same reason I didn't shake him off, the same reason I rotated to face him instead of getting into my car, which was mere feet away at this point.

"No?" he said, then let out an *oomph* when I launched myself into his arms.

"No," I whispered, smothering the groan bubbling up in my throat when those strong arms banded around me, the sensation exactly as I'd imagined . . . that and so much more.

Good.

Great.

What was even better?

His hard cock pressing against my abdomen.

"What's your name?" he asked.

CHAPTER THREE

Archer

MY QUESTION MADE her go stiff in my arms, and I expected her to back away, to step out of my hold. Instead, she surprised me by leaning closer, her pelvis brushing mine.

Pleasure splintered through me when she ground against my cock.

I slid my hand to her hip, pulled her even closer.

"You don't need to know," she murmured, her hand drifting down my side, sliding nearer and nearer to my cock.

"I do if you want me to fuck you."

Her lips parted. Her eyes flashed. "Excuse me?"

I tucked a strand of long brown hair behind her ear. "You heard me."

Brown eyes sparked with fury, and she pushed out of my hold. "Fuck off."

"I'd rather fuck *you*," I said, not grabbing her again, even though I wanted to. This woman had lit a fire in me from the moment I'd seen her close her lips around the beer bottle back at the bar. My cock had twitched. I'd forgotten all about the fact that my shift was over, and I'd studied her closely, committing the planes of her face to memory, trying to ferret out all the different shades of brown in her eyes.

Kace had given me a look, telling me he saw right through my offer of staying on a few extra hours to "help" with the evening crowd, but he hadn't complained or told me to go, he just clapped me on the shoulder and shoved a ticket under my nose.

"Get pouring," he'd said.

I'd poured. I'd watched.

And now, need burned like a living thing within me.

I wanted this woman.

But I needed her to want me, too.

"That's not going to happen," she said on a huff, spinning away.

"Okay," I said. "But you'll think about me when you touch yourself tonight. Think about what we *could* have had," I added, knowing I'd full-well think about *her* when I stroked myself into oblivion. Unless, of course, I could convince *her* to stroke me into oblivion.

I promised I'd stroke her just as good.

She froze, spun back, and lifted her chin. Fuck, but I loved the fire in her brown eyes. "I have no need of a . . ." Her eyes flicked down then back up, a smirk curving her plump lips. ". . . *bartender.*"

Said like I spent the evenings shoveling shit.

Which would be a far more noble job than pouring alcohol and delivering the odd basket of chicken strips.

"Good thing I'm *not* just a bartender."

Her brows arched, brown wings floating up toward her hairline. "Oh yeah?"

I stepped closer. "Yeah."

A snort, almost delicate and musical, mirroring the natural rhythm and grace this woman held. "So, what else are you?"

"I'll tell you if you tell me your name."

Her lips parted, irritation drawing her face into harsh lines. Then she sighed, the lines smoothing out, her hair shifting like a cape behind her as she shook her head. "Goodnight . . . *bartender.*"

She stepped toward her car.

Fuck.

I moved close, smelled vanilla on her skin. "You want me."

She sniffed. "I've got an eight-inch vibrator in my drawer at home, and it won't stop until I'm satisfied."

My lips twitched. "Unless the batteries run out."

I thought I spotted a glimmer of humor in her eyes. "Lucky for me, I'm well stocked."

"I'm not sure if I can deliver on eight inches, but I sure as shit promise to not stop until you're satisfied." Even if it killed me. Hell, I'd look forward to plunging into eternal slumber if that death was wrought by pleasuring this woman.

She scoffed, pretty eyes rolling heavenward. "If I had a penny for every time a man promised that . . ."

"You could already have my cock buried inside you," I murmured. "Already be halfway to satisfied."

Her mouth parted, breath slipping out, coating my lips.

I hadn't been aware of moving, of shifting to be so close, and the temptation of her was almost overwhelming. I could smell vodka and pineapple; knew she'd taste as sweet as I'd first thought.

"Not eight inches?" she breathed, one finger coming to trail over my chest.

And just like that, I was rock hard, moisture beading on the head of my cock. "I don't know," I murmured.

That finger trailed down. "*How* don't you know?"

"I've never measured."

The ghost of a smile. "I promise to let you inside me," she murmured. "I just don't promise to tell you my name."

My dick ached, throbbed to be sinking home, but I had the distinct notion that if I wanted to keep this woman around, I needed to win this battle—or maybe not *this* battle. Perhaps, just *a* battle.

"No name," I agreed, my brain threatening to short circuit, though I managed to at least rub two brain cells together. "But only if you tell me something about yourself no one else knows." Her lips parted, a protest forming on her face, drawing her brows together, sparks in those eyes again. "Something small or big. I don't care."

Silence.

This nameless woman going very, very still.

Her finger flattened out, the palm of her hand pressing to my stomach, trailing lower to the waistband of my jeans. Then she smiled, slipped her fingers just inside that band, brushing the bare skin of my pelvis, dangerously close to my cock.

"Woman," I growled.

"You promise I'll be satisfied?"

"If I have to fuck you until my heart gives out."

Approval softening the lines of her face, creeping into the corners of her eyes, her lips. Then she rose on tiptoe, her breasts flush to my chest, and a groan rumbled up out of my throat. "I crocheted a scarf last week."

It took a moment for her words to process.

Then I grinned, swept my thumb across her bottom lip. "See? Sweet."

Her teeth ground into the digit, sending a sharp spike of desire coursing through me. "Not sweet," she growled before laving the tip of her tongue over my skin.

"Maybe not," I agreed. "But I bet you taste fucking sweet between your thighs."

More teeth.

Then suction.

And for a moment, I worried about my ability to keep my promise of satisfaction.

"Yes?" I asked.

Heat in her eyes, her pupils dilating.

Then she nodded. "Yes."

CHAPTER FOUR

Dominique

"How far is your place?" I asked.

Archer grinned, and it rubbed against my clit like an actual caress . . . or maybe a stroke of his tongue, one I was very much anticipating. "Around the corner. Yours?"

"Your place," I ordered, not bothering to answer that.

Also, yes, *ordered*.

Because my place was a twenty-minute drive away, and I wanted this man sooner than that, and also because I preferred to not invite anyone back to my place if I could help it. Aside from my business and all the important—and private—data I needed to keep safe, I didn't like people in my space.

I was a lone wolf. Separate from the universe. A single, determined tree growing on the top of a mountain. A giant squid propelling myself through the depths of the dark. A—

"My place?" Archer asked, his lips against my throat.

My fingers spasmed, tingles of pleasure zipping through my nerves. "Yes. *Now*."

His husky chuckle joined the tingles, running like fur along the inside of my skin. "My place," he repeated, though this time the statement was accompanied by him wrapping an arm around my waist and guiding me forward.

Unsure if I'd unlocked it, I bleeped my car's key fob, listened to the beep as I searched for any signage that my car wasn't safe here for a few hours.

Not seeing anything other than a sign for street-sweeping that would happen in the early hours of the morning (not a worry, since I'd be long gone by then), I let him lead me down the street and around the corner to a small set of apartments. Then up the stairs with treads that had tiny rocks embedded, the metal railing painted an unattractive brown, down a well-lit hallway, and finally to a stop in front of 2C.

"My place," he said for a third time.

The chill in the air during the short walk had tempered my desire, banking it until the embers glowed deep inside. Definitely not gone but enabling me to have some semblance of brainpower.

"Did you forget how to say anything else, caveman?" I teased as he unlocked the door, reached in, flicked on the lights, then held it wide enough for me to see inside. Bright white walls, a large couch and TV, all typical bachelor accoutrements. The only surprise I could see on that initial inspection was a couple of paintings hung directly opposite the entrance, their colors swirling together in a way that drew the gaze.

They were beautiful.

I wanted.

Which was beside the point because Archer was leaning against the pushed-open door, watching me as I surveyed the space. "What can I say?" he asked. "You fried my ability for competent conversation."

My mouth turned up.

And yet, he could say something like *competent conversation.*

Before I could dwell on that, though, he reached forward and wrapped those long, rough fingers around my wrist—definite shivers to go along with the desire pooling between my thighs. "Pass inspection, Ms. No-Name?"

My mouth turned up further. "I'm impressed you have something hanging on your walls."

He drew me across the threshold, with steady pressure and a hold I could have easily broken. But I didn't *want* to break it. I wanted to be drawn in, to be flush against his body again, to—

"I'll ask you about your other interior design recommendations." He bent and buried his face in my hair. "Later," he added after inhaling deeply. "Fuck, you smell good."

My knees trembled.

Not that I would ever admit such a thing, but they wobbled just the slightest bit at the sound of his voice rasping through the strands of my hair, warming my scalp, skating down my nape. That skating joined the quivering in my thighs, the moisture pooling, soaking my panties. "How about we skip the smelling and get right to the *fuck* part?"

His head lifted, fingers slipping under my chin, tilting it up so I met his stare.

The heat in which nearly melted me into a puddle of goo.

Because it had been a long fucking time since anyone had looked at me with that kind of raw need in their eyes, desire storming through his hazel irises, turning them the color of the damp earth of the forest's floor, bits of sunshine skimming through the clouds and canopy of trees overhead, heating the air . . . and fanning the flames of that fire banked within me.

Then I was in his arms and his mouth was on mine, and for as much as I liked to talk a big game, as much as I'd orchestrated this, had said that I wanted to skip straight to the fucking

. . .

I'd never been kissed like this.

As though I were a passing ship at risk of getting sucked into a whirlpool, circling, circling, *circling,* and then yanked down into oblivion.

He owned my lips, my tongue.

And I had the feeling he was going to own my body in the very same way.

I shivered in delight, in anticipation.

"Cold?" he murmured, setting me on his bed and straightening to tug off my boots and socks.

"Not in the least," I said, my chest heaving, my words coming through rapid gusts of breath.

Archer traced a finger over the arch of my foot, and I jumped, toes clenching. "Tickle?" he asked.

"No." It felt good after my feet had been crammed into boots all night, and what felt better was his rough, warm hands grasping my ankle and digging his thumbs into my arch.

And *that* felt incredible.

He grinned, massaging my foot for several moments before switching to the other, the sensation so fucking amazing that I'd almost willingly trade orgasms for this man's massages.

Almost.

Because then he released my foot, letting it fall to the mattress, and crawled over me. "Sure?" he asked, pausing, his hips on top of mine, pressing into me, letting me feel the hard length of him.

"Do you only speak in one-word questions now?"

He bent, pressed his nose to my throat and inhaled. "So fucking sweet," he growled. He raised his head. "And sometimes you only *need* one word."

"How about two?" I asked. "As in: Fuck. Me."

Archer inhaled sharply.

"Or," I said, reaching between us for the hem of the clingy, silky tank top I wore, "to add a third: *Now.*"

His grin was wicked. "*Now*, I can do." He pushed up, brushed my hands aside, and tugged off my shirt. It flew over his shoulder, landing somewhere behind him, somewhere I didn't track because then his palms were on my stomach, my hips, my sides, sliding center and up . . . and stopping, just below my breasts.

And staying there.

Just *below* my breasts.

For an eternity.

Then one hand shifted, pressed lightly on my sternum while the other slid over my rib cage, slipped under my back, and undid the clasp of my plain black bra. A heartbeat later, his palms were on my breasts, and fuck, that was *good*. Rough callouses on sensitive skin, nerve endings firing on all cylinders.

My nipples grew harder, beading even tighter against his palms, and he brushed back and forth, back and forth, sparking pleasure through me.

"Do you always move so slow?" I complained, needing this man with a desperation that had gripped me tight in its teeth and was shaking me roughly from side to side.

"Slow is good sometimes," he murmured, bending and placing his lips against my skin, dragging them up, bringing them closer and closer to the sensitive bud of my nipple. "Slow can make you feel more." He blew lightly. "Slow can feel better." His tongue darted out.

I gasped.

"Better, see?" he asked, cocky in every letter, and I didn't give a damn because then, as every nerve in my body sizzled and prickled, ached and tensed, he took the bud in his mouth and suckled deeply.

My head fell back, my hips jerked up.

And that was the final movement I was capable of.

Because then he sank heavier against me, pinning me to the bed with his lower half while his hands and mouth, teeth and tongue played my body like an instrument, or maybe like a bundle of nerves, or maybe—

"Archer!" I gasped.

"Not a terrible name when you're moaning it," he said, releasing my nipple, brushing his beard along the underside of my breasts, dragging his mouth across my skin, lower and lower until he reached the button on my jeans.

One flick of his fingers, and it was open.

A tug, and my zipper was down.

Rough fingers reaching into the waistband of my pants, gripping the denim, my underwear, and leaning back to tug them both down at once. They caught on my ankles, and I spent the next few moments trying to kick them off while he stood up and yanked.

"Fucking skinny jeans," I muttered.

"Worth it for the things they do to your ass," he said.

I giggled, using one foot then the other to continue wrestling them down, and eventually, the material slid free, joining my tank top by flying over his shoulder.

And then I was naked.

The raw need in his gaze scorched me.

"You're fucking beautiful," he said, starting to climb back over me.

I put my foot up, rested it against his chest.

He wrapped his hands around my ankle, stroked up my calf, brushed past my thigh, fingers lightly massaging the underside of my ass. "What is it, beautiful?"

"Naked," I ordered, leaving my foot in place even as my hips canted with each touch of his calloused fingertips.

"Yes," he said, those fingers not stopping. "You're gloriously naked."

"And now, I want *you* to be naked," I told him, slipping my leg free and sitting up, reaching for the hem of his T-shirt. "That's how this game works."

"Is it?" He let me tug up his shirt, took over to rip it over his head while I worked on the button of his jeans, the zipper, slipping my hand inside to touch hot, silken skin, velvet-covered steel.

"Yes," I breathed, keeping one hand on his cock, sliding the other around to cup his ass. "Fun, naked time usually involves *both* parties being naked."

"Usually," he agreed, pulling my hands free. "But I don't

think you'd protest if I left my pants on while I fucked you."

Oh.

Oh.

While I was processing that, processing that, no, I wouldn't protest in whatever form he would fuck me, Archer shoved down his jeans and boxer briefs and . . . holy eight inches, Batman. He'd said he wasn't sure he could deliver on the inches, but . . . sweet Christ, the man had a cock that was huge and beautiful and made my lips tingle, desperate to have it sliding between them.

And . . . why not?

I sat up, gripped him, and guided him into my mouth.

CHAPTER FIVE

Archer

I MADE some sort of garbled noise when I slid into the wet heat of this woman's mouth.

"Baby," I groaned, when she wrapped one hand around me, used the other to cup my balls. Pleasure coiled like a spring at the base of my spine, twisting tighter and tighter until I knew that all my talk of satisfying her would be ruined if I didn't get my cock out of her mouth.

Summoning herculean strength, I grabbed her shoulders, set her away from me, tossed her farther up the bed.

Her tits bounced like the most erotic show I'd ever seen, her legs flying wide, giving me a glimpse of wet pink folds, and even though she ordered me to, "Grab a condom," I knew that I had to taste the sweetness of her on my tongue. I pounced, pressing my mouth to her pussy, gliding my tongue through her, finding the bundle of nerves at the apex of her thighs, and taking my time to learn her.

Circling, not direct pressure. Using the flat of my tongue to tease out her sensitive spots, the places that brought her the most pleasure. She squirmed and bucked, tossed her head back, and then her breath hitched.

Her lips parted.

Her thighs clenched.

I didn't stop. I'd sell my soul, lose consciousness, limbs, force my heart to halt beating before I discontinued pleasuring this woman.

"Arch—"

She moaned, hands winding into my hair, grinding against me, and then . . . she screamed.

It was the best sound I'd ever heard, and I held on to her hips, coaxing her through the peak, down the other side, and back up again, avoiding her clit but concentrating gentle and easy strokes until her hands clenched again, until they pulled me closer, until she moaned my name.

Only when her thighs tightened around me, her pelvis bucking once again, this time, I suspected, from sensitivity rather than pleasure, I released her.

"I—" she began.

I climbed up the bed, reaching over her for a condom in the nightstand and finding her lips as I rolled it down my cock.

"Ready?" I asked, needing her to be sure.

In answer, she gripped my ass, tugged me down, and—

I pushed inside.

"Fuck," I groaned.

"Yes," she said, spine arching off the bed, "now."

I took her at her word, starting to move. She was tight and hot, her thighs locked around my waist, the ultimate perfect fit that threatened to undo every part of me. That coil of my control was wound tight, wound beyond what was safe and secure, ready to spring forth at the slightest provocation. I bit the inside of my cheek until I tasted blood but didn't stop moving. And when I found a spot that had her moaning my name, had her pussy clenching around me, I didn't speed, didn't slow, just kept at the rhythm that had her convulsing, curse words tumbling off her tongue, her heels digging into my ass.

"Come for me, sweetheart," I said, or maybe begged, because the edge was right there, tantalizingly close in front of me, and I needed her to orgasm before I burst into flames.

Her voice hitched, and I knew she was close.

Thank fuck, she was close.

Reaching between us, I pressed my thumb to her clit.

And she plummeted, her orgasm washing through her, my cock squeezed tight, pulling me over the edge, sending me plummeting right along with her. Pleasure exploded at the base of my spine, blazing through me, my muscles growing taut and then slack as I collapsed, barely able to get my elbows beneath me so I didn't crush her.

Sweat dripped between my shoulder blades, my abs burned like a motherfucker. I could even feel a foot cramp coming on.

But this had, hands down, been the best sex of my life.

I flopped to the side, chest still heaving, concrete compressing my limbs, dragging them down, making my body lax and limp. By the time I caught my breath, sleep had edged into my brain.

I should move, get up, but I'd just had an orgasm that had nearly blown my spine from my body, so instead I just soaked in the pleasure, the warm woman next to me, the relaxation creeping into me. Hell, it felt like it had been ages since I'd been able to let my guard down with a woman, since I could lie in bed and just . . . be for a couple of minutes.

She rolled to her side, curled up next to me, resting her hand on my chest.

Ice down my spine. Pleasure dissipating to smoke. The real world intruding.

Then she rested her head on my shoulder, traced light patterns over my skin. "You weren't lying," she murmured, the *ing* punctuated with a yawn. "You satisfied, and then some."

I chuckled, rested my hand on her hip. "Glad I lived up to the hype."

"Uh-huh." She nuzzled closer, went still and quiet.

A knot in my chest loosened, one I hadn't even comprehended that I'd held on to . . . well, since May.

Not the month.

My ex-wife.

CHAPTER SIX

Dominique

MY HEAD WAS SPINNING, my heart racing.

And not just from the orgasm . . . the *orgasms*.

This was . . . not a mutually enjoyable night of sex. This was more. And *that* was fucking dangerous. Too fucking dangerous for my blood, despite the gloriousness of this man's cock, despite how lovely it felt to be pressed to his side, his hand draped over my hip, fingers on my ass.

Because I wanted to crawl on top of him, to wake him up, disturb the peaceful sleep he'd fallen into, and have a round two.

But . . . baggage.

I smothered a sigh, closed my heart, despite my senses—the spicy scent of him in my nose, the soft rumbles of his snore, the tingles those fingers sparked along my skin—urging me to stay a little longer.

Instead, I moved in increments. First, lifting his palm from my hip and placing it on his stomach. Which didn't help my temptation.

The man had *abs*.

Just like he had a fantastic cock, a squeezable ass, bulging thighs, and biceps.

I wanted more.

And that was precisely why I had to leave.

If I wanted more and I gave into that temptation . . . well, I'd been down that road, and I knew it only led to pain, heartbreak, and tainted memories. Right now, I had two yummy orgasms, some witty banter, and a single new understanding that I liked drinking Sex on the Beach cocktails. A trifecta of good that I wasn't going to allow to be tarnished by the rest of it.

The rest of it being . . . relationships, connections with other people, and the temptation to see this man again.

So, step two.

Slide out of bed without waking him.

Luckily, even though it had been a while since my sex life had involved anything other than my vibrator friends and me tapping away on my keyboard and pretending that orgasms weren't all they were cracked up to be (a total lie as this man had so effortlessly demonstrated), I had been avoiding pesky links with other human beings for long enough to ensure my sneaking out skills were up to snuff.

Even when those skills involved slowly inching like an earthworm away from the man who'd given me the most incredible orgasm of my life.

Orgasms.

S.

Plural.

Stifling a groan, I searched the room for my clothes. My bra was somehow tucked half under the bed. My jeans were inside out and nearly in the front room. One boot was near a door that must either lead to his closet or bathroom. The other was propped perfectly upright next to the dresser. And my tank was . . . I tilted my head to the side because it was somehow hanging on the doorknob.

The only small victory was that my underwear was still

tangled in my jeans, making it the only item of clothing I didn't have to actively search for.

Go me!

Gathering all of these, I slipped into the front room and got dressed.

Because it was a rookie mistake to do that where the person you were trying to avoid might hear you.

Also, this just in, skinny jeans were the fucking worst.

Great for the FUPA. Excellent for my ass and calves.

Fucking horrible to try to squeeze into post-coitally in a strange apartment when I was trying to silently wrestle denim up my thighs. Eventually, though, I managed to haul them up and over my ass, to button them and yank up the zipper. Next was my bra, my tank, and my boots.

I had a moment of guilt as I walked through the door, but I shoved it away, flicked the lock on my way out, and made my way back down the stairs, fishing my keys out of my pocket as I moved across the parking lot and out onto the street. A few minutes later, I'd turned the corner, spotted my car, and was opening the door.

Then I was *inside* my car, cruising down the freeway to my place, the heat blasting to stave off the chill from my bare arms.

Twenty minutes after that, I was in my house, in my pajamas, and in bed.

But it took many more minutes for me to fall asleep.

And when I finally did, it was with the smell of Archer in my nose, on my skin. The taste of him on my tongue. The feel of him inside me.

———

"FUCK," I whispered. *"Fuck."*

As in, I was so completely, totally fucked.

I was wrestling with my jeans again, trying and searching through the fucking pockets I'd had tailored. The compartments that had held my phone and my car key but didn't hold my wallet.

No matter how deeply I shoved my hand into that specially tailored pocket, my wallet wasn't in there.

So . . . *fuck.*

I thought back to my earthworm tactics from six hours before, tried to picture Archer's bedroom. Was it possible that I missed it having fallen on the floor? Had I lost it somewhere along the way back to my car? Did I—

The doorbell rang.

I glanced up, freezing like a deer who'd been spotted on the side of the road, eyes darting from the jeans in my hand to my computers, which I could see through the open door of my office, taking up almost one entire wall of that space. Technically, it was the bedroom next door, but I'd had the opening installed when I moved in, preferring to stumble out of bed and walk just a few paces to be able to legally (and cough, occasionally *ill*egally) access the data my clients required.

Sometimes it was the government who sought my services.

Sometimes it was a CEO.

Sometimes it was Joe Blow.

But because I had no digital presence outside of my day and evening and sometimes middle of the night job, my clients only came to me via word of mouth. *All* of which meant that I didn't have people dropping by my house at—my eyes flicked to my cell—seven in the morning.

Nope.

No fucking way.

The bell rang again.

I grabbed my phone, pulled up the doorbell camera and, "Aw hell," I muttered when it loaded on my screen.

Archer was standing on my porch, two carafes of coffee in his hands, looking deliciously rumpled, my pussy throbbing in happy memory of his body pressed to mine, his cock driving deep.

His eyes, the color vastly diminished through my cell's screen, flicked toward the camera. "I'm not going anywhere . . . *Dominque*," he said, his voice slightly rasped and sliding over my skin like lace mixed with velvet. He rotated one hand enough for me to see the wallet gripped between the coffee cup and his thumb.

Which answered the question of why he was on my porch.

How he'd found my porch.

Knock. Knock. Knock.

The noise made me jump and I watched as he bent, stared directly into the camera. "I have caffeine. And your wallet, *Dominque*."

And he had my name.

The way he said my name.

Fuck. I was in so much fucking trouble.

I wasn't going downstairs. I wasn't. I couldn't . . . but *God* how I wanted to.

He smiled, and I would swear to the computer gods that I felt it right between my legs, exactly where he'd licked me the night before. "I see how it is," he murmured. "How about I just leave this"—he lifted the hand with the wallet—"here, and I'll just leave?"

"Yes," I muttered. "Just leave."

Archer waited, eyes on the camera. "All right, Niki baby," he said in that soft, rasping voice. "I'll leave."

Then he bent slowly, setting the wallet and the coffee on my doormat and backing slowly off the porch. I watched his retreat through my phone, waited several minutes after he disappeared off the screen, half-expecting him to reappear jack-in-the-box style, popping up out of nowhere and catching me unawares.

I crept downstairs and toward the door, peeked out the window, gaze searching my front yard for any traces of my bearded, hazel-eyed orgasm machine.

But—and I certainly wasn't disappointed—Archer wasn't there.

My fingers flicked the lock, tugged open the wooden panel, slanting another suspicious look at my surroundings, stifling more of that *not* disappointment. The scent of coffee, bitter and roasted, drifted through the air, and I stepped out onto the porch, snatched the cup and my wallet, skidding back inside like a cat darting away from a potential bath, slamming the door, flicking the lock—and checking it twice, for good measure.

Then I took my coffee and my wallet up to my bedroom and crawled back under the covers.

Forget the early start I'd planned.

I was going back to sleep.

CHAPTER SEVEN

Archer

I'D PROBABLY MADE a mistake in not sticking around, but I'd figured that Dominque wouldn't appreciate me pushing her further than I'd already pushed.

The selfishness in me wanted to see her again, to confirm she was as beautiful, as intoxicating to me in the light of the day as she'd been in the apartment the night before.

The rest of me already knew the answer to that.

I had a chubby from a one-sided conversation carried out via a doorbell camera.

So yeah, I already knew I had it bad.

And she'd left before the sun had risen.

She'd *left* approximately thirty minutes after I'd come inside her. I'd heard the door shut, its *click* jarring me out of the sleep I'd sunk into, the condom around my half-hard dick, my bed empty, my heart . . . *sliced.*

It had no right to be feeling anything, sliced open or aching or hurt because she hadn't hung around.

It should be happy to have had some great sex, glad to have found some peace post-May, and ready to get back to my art, my job, my life that didn't involve lusting after a woman, who clearly didn't want anything further to do with me.

One night.

Some fun.

A great orgasm.

Done.

I glanced behind me, checking for traffic as I pulled onto the freeway, making my way back to my house. I was in the middle of a piece, was itching to get back to it, that itch in my fingertips to have it completed. I could feel the smooth wood of the paint-brush's handle on my skin, the rough bite of the canvas, the cool stroke of the colors mixing together getting on my hands as often as the canvas.

I was a messy painter.

But I was a messy painter who'd built a career.

And one who worked in a bar.

Grinning as I navigated through the rush hour traffic, part because May would hate that, and there was nothing I loved more at this point in my life than pissing off my ex-wife (Petty? Yes. Absolutely. But after the hell that she-devil of a woman had put me through, I was embracing the petty. It sure as fuck was better than going to jail for murder). Aside from making May angry, I was working at Bobby's because Kace had asked, because I was new in town, needed a fresh start, and it wasn't like my personal life was hopping. I had nothing to do most evenings except binge documentaries and fantasy shows on Netflix. And drink.

I'd done a lot of drinking over the last six months since the divorce was final.

Of course, it would have been a hell of a lot easier if I could paint at night.

But I was a morning person. Always had been, always would be. I worked best under natural light when the sun was rising, and I painted in a flurry until the clock struck about three, that big ball of gas having crossed the midpoint of the sky and begun its downward descent.

Then I showered, and for the last few months, I'd gone to Bobby's to help with the dinner rush, leaving to head home and crash, to sleep until the sun rose and I began painting all over again.

I was one of the lucky ones with a nest egg, with galleries that actually wanted my work, with money in my checking account.

I had less than May did.

But the prenup we'd signed had meant that I'd kept the rights to my work . . . along with turning down any alimony.

I hadn't needed it.

My life was small and simple and fine.

I didn't need what May did.

And if there was ever a perfect description for my relationship with my ex, it was that.

What I wanted and what my ex wanted had been on two different planes of existence.

Sighing, I parked and got out of my car, making my way up to my apartment and into the kitchen, where I fueled up quickly on a bagel and another cup of coffee—caffeine was part of my process. When I was nearing jittery, I placed my mug in the sink, changed into my paint-stained clothes, and slipped into the second bedroom.

Most people would have a guest room.

With just my brother, who lived a busy life and didn't visit often, my friends nearby with their own nicer places, I had no need for a guest room.

I did, however, have need of a painting studio, and one with bright, natural light. This bedroom, with its eastern-facing window, was a big part of the reason I'd signed the eighteen-month lease. That and being on the top floor and in the corner of the complex.

Quiet.

No loud neighbors clomping overhead.

Today I glanced out my window as I slanted open the blinds, focused on the final selling point. The park in the distance.

Which . . . now that I thought about it, made me sound like the worst type of person, creeping on people in the park. But my art wasn't like that. I started with an image that inspired me. Sometimes a tree changing colors. Sometimes, like this morning, a trio of dogs in mismatched sizes frolicking along the path. Sometimes a kid hanging upside down on the monkey bars, pigtails sailing in the wind.

And I tried to capture the spirit of that moment.

The mix of courage, exhilaration, and fear as she let go of the green metal to dangle by her knees.

The joy in the prancing pooches' steps, their noses pointed into the wind, their tails on full propellor mode.

The bleakness that sometimes accompanied a season changing—trees going bare, their limbs naked and frail—but hope coiled in the background, winding tight and preparing to spring forth in the form of green buds and leaves unfurling.

My mind clear except for those dogs, I pulled out a fresh canvas, slapped paint onto my palette, grabbed a brush, and began.

No sketching beforehand.

Those pencil lines stymied me, faint markings that boxed me in instead of allowing me the freedom I needed to create.

I needed paint on the canvas, I needed to not overthink, and I needed the sun shining in through my window as I worked.

And while normally, the image I'd spotted would stay in my mind, fueling that creativity for however many hours I stayed in my almost trancelike state, painting furiously, today the vision morphed, twisted, transformed.

Into brown hair and eyes.

Into a plump mouth and exposed shoulders that called out to be kissed.

Into a lush ass and thighs wrapped around my waist and a tongue in my mouth.

Minutes turned into hours, and the next time I was aware of anything, the light had dimmed. I'd blown by my usual afternoon stop time and had drifted into evening.

My feet were sore. My shoulders ached. My hands were cramping.

But I looked at my canvas, and I saw . . . Dominque.

Oh, I was so fucked.

CHAPTER EIGHT

Dominque, a month later

I was going to kill Hayden.

Seriously murder him.

Or at least hack into his records and leak his personal information on the Dark Web so that anyone with dubious morals could access it.

Except, there was a reason I'd hired the fucker, and that was because he was good. So it would probably be a pain in the ass to get through his encryptions and firewalls, and I really tried to avoid doing things that were a pain in the ass.

At least when I wasn't paid to do them.

But the fucker . . . he'd promised that Archer wouldn't be here.

But the fucker (Archer this time) *was* here.

And I'd given up information—that I had an interest in avoiding the bearded, hazel-eyed mass of yumminess—to Hayden with absolutely no return on that investment. Hayden's interest was spiked, and now Archer was setting a glass that appeared to contain a Sex on the Beach in front of me, his rumbling voice rolling across my skin like a thunderstorm.

My nipples went hard, my pussy went damp, and I squirmed on the stool like I'd broken my tailbone when all I'd really done was broken my most important rule when it came to sleeping with this man.

I knew better.

My rule was in place because I knew that nothing good came from sleeping with men who I actually liked, who liked me, who wanted more than just mutual orgasms.

I needed to keep my distance. Stay safe.

But I hadn't, had I?

Because soon he'd want things I couldn't give, and then he wouldn't be shining his sexy smile in my direction now, would he?

Of course, I thought, my heart leaping in my chest like a Labrador puppy, I'd also gone and broken another rule. One just as important. Because I'd started to like the fucker back. Because I couldn't deny that a bubble of something swelled inside me—a tennis ball for that wriggling puppy to chase—when he rested his elbows on the bar and asked, "Hungry, sweetheart?"

I pushed the glass away, even though I had saliva building up, my taste buds prickling at the memory of the mix of tart and sweet on my tongue, my body ready for the glorious buzz of vodka to hit my veins.

I'd actually bought the supplies to make this drink, but my home concoctions didn't taste nearly as good as when this man had made it.

I wanted to grab the glass, to feel its damp cold seep into my fingertips, to trace patterns in the condensation, to grip the thin straw and bring it up to my lips, sucking deeply.

I *wanted* to suck something else deep.

But . . . rules.

And I'd broken enough of them already to know that I couldn't break the most important of them.

Having another night with Archer.

Instead of acknowledging him, I turned to Hayden and continued our conversation. The project was nearly complete, and the bar with its background music and din of people joking and laughing, drinking and talking, was an easy place to haggle out those final few details.

Hayden was sent on his way with plans to let himself into a few high-powered servers and report his findings.

It would likely take him all night, but if they were clean, then I could report to KTS that the person they had us investigating wasn't connected to their criminal ring.

We'd have a couple of days off and then move onto the next project.

Which, if I was remembering correctly, would be trying to uncover information to prove whether a powerful CEO was cheating on his wife (soon-to-be ex-wife) so she had materials for the divorce proceedings.

Look, not all of my life could be noble or glamorous.

The majority of it involved me squinting at a screen, seeing shit I couldn't *unsee*, and then really hating my job.

The minority, the piece that kept me going, aside from the fact that I'd fought tooth and nail for it, had clawed myself into financial independence and forced my way into a seat at the table was that sometimes I did *real* good.

Sometimes we helped in ways that didn't involve divorce decrees or clearing people who weren't particularly squeaky clean but who hadn't committed bad enough crimes to be the big fish we were after. *Sometimes* we found kids who were missing and were able to reunite families. Sometimes I found money that was stolen and was able to shift some things around and have it magically make its way back into the proper accounts. Sometimes I caught evidence on cameras or in emails and was able to pass it onto police forces to solve outstanding cases.

Those were the reasons that kept me moving forward.

Despite all the things I couldn't unsee.

Tonight, however, Hayden clapped me on the shoulder, pushed off his stool, and moved to the other end of the bar, to his gorgeous Anabelle, and left me with a drink full of rapidly melting ice.

"Here."

I blinked, tearing my gaze away from the sunset in my glass and allowing it to rise, to meet Archer's.

"Here," he said again, sliding a basket across the bar in front of me.

It wasn't fancy or anything particularly special, a sampler of fried bar foods—chicken strips, mozzarella sticks, wings, a bit of celery and carrots to pretend to be healthy, and a trifecta of dipping sauces.

"No," I said, shoving it away, even as my stomach rumbled.

He steadied it, his slow grin burning through me. "Sounds like your stomach thinks differently."

He tapped the wood, straightened, and moved a few feet away, pulling glasses out of a dishwasher and stacking the blue plastic racks behind him.

It was his biceps.

Later, I'd blame his biceps.

They strained against the cotton of his shirt, veins crossing the bulging muscles, making my mouth water. I'd tasted his skin, could remember the notes of spice, how it had become tinged with salt when he'd thrust with the drive of a man who wasn't going to stop until he'd brought me over the edge.

Until I'd been . . . satisfied.

I shivered . . . and caught his eyes in the mirror.

Fire and need and the temptation to break all my rules just so I could have this man be mine. For only a few minutes. For more. For—

Fucking hell, I picked up one of the mozzarella sticks and bit into it.

Salt and goo—

Which was really not helping me with the whole not fucking

Archer thing. *Barf.* Especially when I was trying to avoid looking at him. *Failing* avoiding looking at him. Because the man had . . . paint . . . on the back of his arm. A smear of bright blue along his triceps.

He turned, caught me looking, and though I dropped the fried bit of mozzarella like it was a stick of dynamite, the fucker saw it anyway.

His eyes sparkled with humor, his mouth turning up.

I wanted to punch him. I wanted to kiss him.

So, back to the whole *fucking hell* thing.

But also, fuck the *fucking hell*, fuck me worrying about that man and his gorgeous body, his wonderful cock. I had a basket of fried deliciousness in front of me, and I was going to clog my arteries.

A.K.A. I was going to eat it.

Without regret and without paying the least bit of attention to the person my body was paying the *most* attention to.

See? That made total sense.

Also, this just in, it made absolutely no sense.

I picked up another mozzarella stick anyway.

CHAPTER NINE

Archer

I FELT the moment that Dominque left.

As though all the nerves in my body had been singularly attuned to her, and now that she was gone, they were signaling to me, telling me to go after her.

But I had work to do.

I began racking glasses. Next, I'd need to check for what alcohol was low, and I was pretty sure there was a keg that was about to run out, and—

A hand on my arm.

"Go after her."

I glanced down, saw that Anabelle had come up next to me.

"What's up?" I asked.

She nudged me back. "Don't play stupid. Go after her."

"Go after who?"

A sigh. "Archer, so help me God, I will squirt lime juice in your eye. That woman wants you."

"She's given me firm *Do Not Proceed* signs."

"So, she's going to make you work for it," Anabelle said. "The best things in life are worth working for. Plus, she's spent the majority of the evening eye-fucking you, so it's not like she's immune."

"Still, that doesn't mean I should—"

"It's dark out. She's walking to her car *in the dark*."

My hands convulsed on the rack of glasses, remembering the last time she'd gone off, how that little fuck boy had cornered her. What if someone else did the same? What if—

"Go," Anabelle said. "You're off anyway."

I'd been late after my painting had run long. Again. I'd been so wrapped up in Dominque, in painting her in different shapes and formats and colors (also yes, I was aware that this was bordering on obsessive, but I hadn't painted this efficiently in years), that I'd come late to my shift. Again.

Good thing I was just doing Kace a favor.

Because I'd seriously be fired if I wasn't.

Still, I'd always stayed after, working off the time I'd missed, even if it was just scrubbing dishes in the kitchen or cleaning up the storeroom.

Today, though, with the thought of Dominque walking into trouble, or trouble finding her, I untied my apron, dropped it on the counter behind the bar, and I left, pushing through the crowd as I searched for any sign of the curvy brunette.

There wasn't a glimpse of her in the hall or in the front room, nor in the area immediately in front of Bobby's.

I glanced around, still looking, then turned in the direction she'd parked before, some instinct driving me to at least try to see where she was, to make sure she was good, and maybe just to get one more glimpse of her before she turned into smoke again. Because I had the feeling that she wouldn't be coming back to the bar.

I stepped off the curb, prepared to cross the street. I'd go one more block and—

"Watch out!"

A body slammed into mine.

A car flew by, close enough that I felt the heat of its engine sear my face.

We hit the concrete hard, the air whooshing out of me, pain radiating through my arms, my ass, my head. My teeth clinked together, spots flashing on the edges of my vision.

"Are you okay?" Dominque asked, her hands on my chest, her legs straddling my torso.

I sat up, one hand around her waist, blinking as my brain struggled to process the last few moments. "I'm fine," I said, gently pushing her off me, standing, and helping her to her feet. I cupped her cheek. "Are you?"

Her lips parted, a breath shuddering out. Then her expression went fierce, and she smacked my chest. "What's wrong with you?" she exclaimed. "You could have been killed!" Another smack. "You were nearly run over and—" Her eyes widened. "You're bleeding!"

"Niki," I murmured.

Soft fingers encircled my wrists, and she turned my hands over, studying them. "You're bleeding, Arch."

"I'm fine—"

She slipped her arm around my waist, started tugging me down the sidewalk.

"What are you doing?" I asked, stumbling slightly. My vision was a little hazy, and my head throbbed like a motherfucker.

"Taking you back to your place."

I smiled.

"Not like that," she snapped, hauling me to a stop at the corner, pausing to deliberately look both ways.

We crossed the street, and I opened and closed my mouth a few times, shrugged my shoulders, rolling my neck. The haze began to clear, the ache fading away. I'd had my cage rattled courtesy of Dominque's tackle, but I hadn't been run over by a car, so that was something.

I walked alongside her to my apartment, appreciating the

sensation of her pressed to my side but not daring to do anything about it lest she leave my ass on the curb.

"Keys," she ordered.

I pulled them out of my pocket, handed them to her. She unlocked the door, held it for me, and then she gripped my hands.

"Where's the bathroom?"

I nodded toward my bedroom.

She hauled me forward, through my bedroom and into the bathroom, shoving me to sit on the edge of the tub. "Stay," she ordered.

I stayed as she began rummaging through my cupboards and drawers.

"Feel free to snoop."

A narrow-eyed gaze in my direction.

I shut my mouth.

She opened the cabinet beneath the sink, pulled out the first aid kit I kept there, along with a washrag. Then she spent the next ten minutes doing something I never would have expected —fussing. So much fussing over my hands, over the back of my head, over my elbows, my palms. She wet the rag, cleaned out the abrasions, checked my head for lumps.

And all the while she *tsked* and muttered, checking every inch of exposed skin before pulling up my T-shirt and stroking a hand up my back.

"What are you doing?"

"Looking for bruises."

"If you want my shirt off, just ask."

She leaned back in front of me, more eye narrowing happening. "Archer," she muttered, "so help me God, I will—"

"I've already been threatened with lime juice tonight," I said. "That's a good one."

A long, suffering sigh.

"Niki?"

She froze.

I caught her wrist, pressed a kiss to her palm. "Thank you."

Her lips parted, breath slipping out, and she was near enough that I felt it caressing my mouth.

"You need to watch where you're going," she said. Another order, though this one was tempered, her tone gentled. Her fingers sifted through my hair. "You scared the shit out of me."

"Sorry," I murmured and drew her closer, until she sank down into my lap, and I wrapped my arms around her waist.

"For the record," she said into my hair. "I shouldn't give two shits about you getting run over on a dark street corner."

I chuckled. "Noted."

But she was letting me hold her, so I wasn't going to complain.

My body's awareness of her grew, my cock remembering that it was near where it'd had a great time a month before, my fingers itching to sketch, to capture the fierceness that had been in her eyes when she'd snapped at me for not paying attention, my lips aching to taste her again.

Eventually, though, she sighed and pushed out of my hold.

Disappointment swelled. I knew she would be leaving, but as much as I wanted her, as much as I'd thought about her over the last month, as much as I felt this intense, persistent connection to her, Dominque didn't owe me anything.

I stood. "I'll walk you to your car."

She went still. Then rotated back to face me, her hands on her hips. "What are you talking about?"

"You're getting ready to leave," I said. "I'll walk you to your car."

"What makes you think that?"

I shrugged. "I guess . . . because you're standing and heading for the door."

Silence. Then, "I was going to make you a cup of coffee."

I blinked. "It's nearly ten."

The barest hint of pink appeared on her cheeks. "It's the only thing I know how to make besides sundaes."

Laughter bubbled in my chest. "Coffee and sundaes sound like a good combination." I stepped closer, tucked a strand of hair behind her ear. "Also, it just so happens that I have the fixin's for both."

"Fixin's?" she asked, not backing away, even when I pressed closer.

"Yup." My mouth drifted to hers, pausing with the barest millimeter of space between our lips. "*Fixin's.*"

"Mmm." A beat. "How's your head?"

My brows drew together. "Fine."

"And your arms?"

"Also fine."

"And your—"

"Every part of me is fine."

Her eyes, deep pools of melted chocolate, sparkled with laughter. That same laughter also bubbled out of her lips, filling the air with the lovely tinkling sound of her amusement. "Okay, well, Mr. Everything is Fine"—she wound her arms around my shoulders—"do you feel *fine* enough for me to make you sundaes and coffee?"

Even if I'd been a broken, useless heap, I would have found the strength to be fine enough to do anything for this woman.

Which was why I took her hand and led her to the kitchen.

CHAPTER TEN

Dominque

I SMACKED Archer's hand away. "I *said*, no touching!"

He laughed and leaned a hip against the counter, his smile a bright flash of white in the dim light of the kitchen. "I didn't think it was possible for someone to truly summon the power of a tornado inside."

Studying my work, I scooped out some more chocolate ice cream and plunked it into Archer's bowl. Perfect. He was a big man, needed to have plenty of calories to fuel those delicious thighs. As to why I had the same amount of ice cream in *my* bowl, well, I'd worked hard that evening by pushing him out of the path of an oncoming car and tending to his wounds—cough, scrapes—so that definitely required extra calories courtesy of ice cream.

I set the scoop on the counter, picked up the can of whipped cream, and began spraying it on my confection. "I don't know what you're talking about."

He picked up the scoop, used a paper towel to wipe beneath it, before placing it in the sink. "You equal tornado."

I made a face. "You're one of those, aren't you?"

"One of what?"

"A neat freak."

He clamped his hand to his chest, pretended to stagger back. "You wound me with such rhetoric."

I sprayed more whipped cream, and yeah, maybe I got a bit on the counter. So what?

Archer swooped in, snagged the can from me, and snapped on the lid, returning it to the fridge, before coming back and wiping up my mess. "Aside from strongly believing in the healing qualities of cleaning, I don't like to touch sticky shit."

I chuckled. "No, you don't like to get your hands dirty."

He snorted.

"What?"

He ignored my question, asked, "Do I get hot fudge on my sundae? Cherries, nuts, and sprinkles?"

Since it was furthering my consumption of ice cream calories, I picked up the bottle of hot fudge, drizzled it over both bowls, and paused because I'd spilled a few drops outside the bowls.

Drops.

Blobs.

What was the difference?

He snagged the bottle, wiped the top.

I smothered a smile and went to work on the cherries, the nuts, the sprinkles. "You know what you need?" I asked, deliberately dropping a few of the nonpareils onto the counter, just to see what he would do.

"What?" he asked, sweeping them into his hand and walking them to the trash can, dumping them in.

"A robot vacuum."

He laughed. "Or a sundae maker who doesn't delight in torturing me." He dipped a finger in the bowl—

"Hey, that's mine!" I exclaimed, batting him away. "Hands off the—"

He painted the whipped cream, syrup, and ice cream mixture over my lips.

I shuddered.

Fucking hell.

Then his lips were on mine, and his tongue was in my mouth, and I forgot all about tormenting him with sprinkles and hot fudge. Instead, I just pressed closer and sank into the kiss. Chocolate and spice, sweet on my tongue, heat against my front, hands in my hair, a hard cock against my stomach.

I moaned, jumped slightly, totally forgetting about his scrapes until I was already in his arms, but thankfully they didn't seem to be bothering him because he grasped on to my thighs, coaxed them around his hips, and turned to set me on the kitchen table. Hard wood on my spine. A chair getting kicked out of the way, and then Archer on top of me.

One hand slipped under my shirt, cupped my breast, teased my nipple, and, all the while, he continued kissing me, whipping my desire into a frenzy.

I grabbed any part of him I could—his arms, his ass, his hair, his face. I yanked at his shirt, and he broke the kiss long enough to tear it off, leaned back enough to step out of his jeans, to work on mine.

"Why in the fuck do you keep wearing these fucking torture contraptions?" he muttered, lifting my hips, yanking them down my legs, tearing them off along with my sneakers. They hit the floor with a soft *th-wump*, and he yanked off my panties, tugged me toward the edge of the table, dropped to his knees.

"Oh fuck," I breathed as he pressed his mouth to me.

He groaned, the vibration sliding through me. His tongue and teeth and lips worked together, teasing me to a precipice in an unbelievably short amount of time. He slipped a finger inside, reached up to roll a nipple between his fingers.

And I exploded, my orgasm rolling through me in tsunami after tsunami. My lungs sawed, my body was covered in sweat, my limbs limp. "Archer," I moaned.

"I'm here," he said, grasping my hand.

"Inside me."

Hard muscles, a sharp inhale.

And then he moved, and I watched him through hooded eyes as he bent for his jeans, extracted his wallet, and pulled out a condom.

A crinkle.

He rolled it down the length of his cock and stepped between my legs.

And pushed home.

I moaned at that first pleasure-pain of him sinking in, then again when he bottomed out, his hips meeting my thighs, his cock deep inside me.

"Good?" he asked.

I knew he was checking in with me, making sure I was fine, but that wasn't the question I answered, what had me arching my back, my pelvis tilting to take him deeper. Instead, my, "Yes" was in reply to the wonderful feelings, the incredible sensations, the fury of need and pleasure that was intertwined within me.

Somehow Archer knew that, and he chuckled, pulling out slowly, driving back in, driving me, slow and steady, back up the cliffside. And just like before, it didn't take any effort to find our rhythm, to move together in a way that would send us flying in no time at all.

Sweat gathered between my breasts, his rough hands filled my nerves with sensation. I was close again. Already.

I wrapped my legs around him, held him tight, and when he murmured my name, his hand coming to my ass, tilting me for an even better angle, I came, convulsing around him, riding those tsunamis once more, and knowing that I'd done something both incredible and stupid.

Because the invisible string tying me to this man had just grown exponentially stronger.

———

HE HADN'T FALLEN ASLEEP this time.

And I'd made a critical error in allowing myself to get carried away with this man while he was fully awake.

Case in point, he'd lifted me, carrying me to the bathroom, setting me on the counter next to him while he washed up and took care of the condom. He snagged a bathrobe off the back of the door, slipping it around me.

See? Awake.

And doing things that made me all melty.

Maybe I could hit him over the head with the . . . soap dispenser. Knock him out, get dressed, and run again.

"You can't knock me out with that puny thing," he said. "It's cheap plastic."

I narrowed my eyes. "Want to bet?"

"No." After bopping me on the nose, he stepped into his closet, pulled on a pair of boxer briefs, before crossing to me and stepping between my thighs. "But if you do"—he leaned in, put his lips to my ear—"you'll never find where I hid your skinny jeans."

I laughed, despite myself. "Um, except, you didn't actually hide them, just tossed them on the floor."

A shrug. "Maybe."

"No maybe about it." I pushed him back then slid off the counter, trying to ignore that he reached for me to ease me down, his warm hands gripping my arms. "I saw them en route. For such a neat freak, you sure don't care where you toss my clothes."

A husky chuckle. "I promise to fold them later . . . if you're around later." There was the barest hint of challenge in his hazel eyes.

"No guarantees."

He bent again, nipped my ear. "Okay then." He straightened. "Let's move. Your ice cream is melting."

I narrowed my eyes. "I'm only staying until I've had my sundae."

"What about my coffee?" he asked, tugging a strand of my hair. "I thought you promised to make me a cup."

My fingers brushed the doorjamb as I left the bathroom, padding with bare feet across the carpet of his bedroom, making my way across the kitchen and picking up my bowl. And then squirting some extra fudge on top, just for good measure.

Archer's voice hit my ears, shimmering down my spine, streaking between my thighs. "No coffee?"

I huffed, glared at him over my shoulder, but I stomped to the pot, banged around his cabinets until I found the coffee and mugs, and set the machine brewing. "You think you're funny, don't you?"

"Nope," he murmured, having picked up his own bowl. He held two spoons in his other hand, lifted his brows. "Very *not* funny," he added, even though the fucker was stifling a smile.

More stomping.

This time over to grab a spoon, snag my bowl, and using both to facilitate shoving ice cream into my mouth.

Archer moved next to me, snaking an arm around my waist and sitting down in one of the kitchen chairs with me in his lap.

"What are you doing?" I asked archly.

"Sitting," he said, holding the bowl in front of me and scooping from it. "Eating."

I huffed.

He chuckled, and the warm breath on my nape mixed with the cold ice cream in my mouth, a shiver wracking through my body. Archer just pulled me closer, lifted his spoon again.

After a few moments, I managed to relax enough to eat my own sundae, the sugar hitting my taste buds, my bloodstream, steadying my anxiety.

The coffee pot hissed and bubbled, the bitter, roasted smell wafting up to my nose, and I found myself studying his space with interest and curiosity rather than going for a quick exit. He had that gorgeous pair of paintings on his far wall, an intriguing mix of colors and shapes taking up most of the space. Near them, another door was half-open, the lights off, and the shadows inside not revealing much of anything. Shifting, I glanced over my other shoulder, saw the brown leather couch, the large TV from before. Though, he had throw pillows and blankets on the surface, making it appear cozy. Like a place I'd want to curl up and watch a show.

The thought of curling up anywhere with someone I'd fucked made an actual cold sweat break out on my spine.

But before I could work myself up into a real tizzy, Archer stood, lifting me out of his lap and setting me on the chair, then crossed to the coffee pot, pouring two mugs. "Cream or sugar?"

"Black," I whispered.

"So, I guessed right the other day."

Guessed right a month before.

Thirty-one days of me thinking about him too much, about that night, about what might have happened if I'd answered the door.

He set a mug in front of me then took our empty bowls to the sink and began washing up. I watched unabashedly, convenient since the task lent itself to him keeping his back to me.

"Neat freak," I muttered after drooling over his biceps for a few minutes.

"And proud of it."

I sniffed, stood, started wandering around as I slowly sipped my coffee. I should have left. I'd announced it just fifteen minutes before. Staying was breaking the rules. But instead of leaving, I found myself moving toward the paintings on the far side of the room, drawn into the colors and the swirling brush strokes.

"Snooping?" he asked.

I glanced over my shoulder, saw he'd picked up our discarded clothes and was folding them. "You said I could."

"True." That done, he moved onto wiping down the counters.

I turned back around, studied the canvases.

They really were quite stunning.

"Who . . ." I trailed off, the question poofing away when I caught a glimpse of what was behind that half-open door.

"Niki?" he asked.

Too distracted to answer, I took my snooping to the next level, pushed into the room, and flicked on the lights.

CHAPTER ELEVEN

Archer

I'D BEEN HAPPILY SCRUBBING hot fudge from my granite when I caught the flicker of light out of the corner of my eye.

Fuck.

I spun just in time to see her disappear into my studio. Tossing down the towel and hurrying across the room, I instantly knew what she'd see and how it would appear.

Canvas after canvas of *her*.

The slopes of her shoulder.

Her mouth. Her eyes. Her hair.

It had become nearly obsessive, and with me painting her over and over again. But even with all that practice, I hadn't managed to capture her . . . essence. That was elusive, just out of reach.

Something else that would be elusive?

Dominque.

Because she couldn't even commit to a couple of hours together; what the hell was she going to do with thirty-plus canvases with her likeness on them?

Run.

Run fast. Run like hell. Run without ever looking back.

And, truthfully, I couldn't blame her.

If I'd stumbled upon some weird-ass shrine erected and fawning over me, over my various body parts, from ears to mouth, from breasts to calves . . . I'd fucking run, too.

"Niki," I murmured, and she glanced up from my main work easel, from the newest piece I was working on, meeting my eyes for the barest moment before she spun slowly, taking in the canvases stacked, sometimes five deep, on the floor. She moved to one such pile, propped the first painting forward, paused as she studied the one behind and behind, until she'd made her way through the entire stack.

Another glance at me.

And then she moved to the next pile. Then the next and the next and the next, until she'd made her way around my entire studio, taking in every painting while I stood there helpless, thinking desperately for anything I might say that would make this seem less creepy.

But nothing came to mind.

So, I just stood in the doorway silently watching her, kicking myself because that was also creepy.

Finally, she finished her circle and stopped in front of me.

"You have paint on your arm."

I opened my mouth. Closed it. "I—"

Her fingers brushed a spot on my left triceps, and I glanced down, saw the streak of blue. "Hazard of the job, unfortunate-ly," I said. "No matter how hard I try to be neat."

"Hmm."

She moved away again, stopped in front of the easel. "You're very good," she murmured.

My lips parted. "I . . . thanks."

"You painted those pieces in the front room?"

I nodded.

"They're beautiful."

An exhale. Maybe she hadn't realized that a lot of the paintings were of her? I hadn't painted her entire face, just silhouettes and profiles and close-ups of different body parts. "Thanks," I said again, relaxing marginally.

She drifted back, her gaze dragging along the canvases. "Is there a reason that a vast majority of them are of me?"

I froze, that respite of calm disappearing.

Of course, she'd noticed, and she was prepared to run if my answer wasn't up to snuff, if the expression on her face was any indication.

"Yes," I said, knowing I could lie or tell the truth.

Knew that, really, I only had one choice.

I had to tell her the truth.

Inhaling deeply and releasing it slowly, I said, "They're all of you because I've spent the last month dreaming of you, reliving our night together, remembering the way your lips, your skin, your body felt." Moving toward her, I cupped her cheek. "I've spent nearly every waking moment trying to recapture that magic. But no reproduction can even begin to compete with the reality."

I felt her throat spasm as she swallowed. "You realize how that all sounds," she murmured, "don't you?"

"I do." I let my hand fall to my side. "Why do you think I haven't been back to your place, sweetheart? I knew if I even allowed myself to consider the possibility that I might see you again, I'd approach stalker level."

"More so than painting my likeness in no less than several dozen different forms?"

That was a fair point.

"Yes."

Her lips turned up at the corners.

"I like you, Niki," I said. "More than I should, and I want to fall in, want to dive deep and learn everything about you. I also know that me telling you that is going to send you running for the door." I blew out a breath. "Which is why I didn't go to your house, why I didn't ask Anabelle to get your number from

Hayden. Instead, I painted." I moved toward one of the canvases, picked it up, holding it out. "And *this* is why I painted."

She took the canvas, colorful splashes of me attempting to capture the rich browns of her irises, and studied it for several long moments.

Then she set it down.

A heartbeat later she was out of the room.

"Fuck," I whispered, waiting for her to get dressed, to then hear the front door open and close, but when long minutes passed and I didn't, I let my chin fall to my chest, knowing she'd gone, but I just hadn't heard her leave.

It was the logical conclusion.

I'd told her the reason her features were plastered on every scrap of canvas in my studio, and logically, she'd gone. Because the draw I felt toward Dominque was intense, and it didn't make sense, and . . . she'd made it clear that she didn't do connection.

Why would she be tempted into furthering a fledging link with a man she didn't know?

I flicked off the light, slipped out of the room, and closed the door behind me. I'd finish cleaning, go to bed, and in the morning, I'd try to excise her from my head. I'd paint however many fucking canvases it took.

And then I'd move on.

I sprayed down the table, rinsed the coffee pot and mugs, grabbed my stack of clothes. Then checked that the front door was locked, the lights were off, before going into the bedroom . . . and stopping in my tracks.

My bed wasn't empty.

Instead, there was a beautiful woman tucked under the sheets, her bare shoulders gilded in the moonlight, her hair down and tumbling around her like a shining brown cape.

"What are you doing?"

She held up the remote. "Getting ready to watch a movie."

"I—uh—"

She patted the bed. "You going to get in?"

"You didn't go?"

"You're making me *want* to." Her mouth curved.

Since I didn't want *that*, I hustled across the room and crawled under the blankets, feeling strangely out of sorts, considering it was my bed. As it was, I held my breath when I wrapped my arm around her, half-expected my hand to pass right through, as though she were an apparition and not a real woman.

"What do you want to watch?"

Her eyes sparkled and she cuddled up next to me, her palm on my chest. "Porn."

I choked on my tongue, first from the cuddling then again from her matter-of-fact declaration.

She laughed, the sound filling my blood with helium. Without the heft of the blankets, without the weight of her body curling up on me, I might have just floated up to the ceiling.

She shifted, resting her head against my chest, her gaze on the TV as she flicked through the menu of a streaming service.

"Did I break you?" she murmured.

"Yes."

More laughter. A pat on my chest. "You'll be fine."

Quiet fell as she put on an action flick, and we watched in silence for several minutes, but then I found myself breaking it, finding a question bubbling in my throat and escaping. "Why did you stay?"

She went still then paused the movie, studied my face.

I held her gaze.

Eventually, Niki relaxed. "Because I wanted to," she said, poking me. "You got a problem with that?"

"No."

A narrowed-eye glare. "You going to use my blood to make new paintings?"

"No." A beat. "However, I *was* planning on creating new canvases with your skin."

She settled back down. "Well, if it's *just* that." Then promptly lifted back up, hitting me with the glare again. "This doesn't mean anything, and I'm only staying for the movie, and maybe some more sex."

I lifted my hands in surrender, feeling like I'd won a battle I hadn't even fought in. "Duly noted." She hit play; the sound of gunshots and explosions, curse words and tires squealing filled the room.

But I didn't watch the movie.

Instead, I watched her.

And it was infinitely more enjoyable than the film.

———

I WOKE to empty arms and sunlight slanting through the windows.

I inhaled, smelled the sweet spice of Niki on the air, on my pillows, my skin. The bed next to me was still warm, meaning that she'd been with me at least part of the night.

Progress.

Of a sort.

Because I still woke up alone.

Sighing, I pushed out of bed, wandered into the front room, was drawn into the kitchen, where the smell of coffee filled the air.

I saw the cup steaming on the counter the same time I heard the door *click* closed.

Bypassing the tempting brew, I hurried to the door, opened it, and saw the top of Dominque's head disappearing down the stairs.

"Coward!" I called.

"Put some pants on, Archer," she called back.

I glanced down, realized that I, indeed, wasn't wearing

pants, and as tempted as I was to chase after her, getting arrested for indecent exposure wasn't on my list of things to do.

"I'll see you soon, Niki!"

"No, you won't." A beat. "Also, my name is Dominque!"

My lips curved. "*Soon*, sweetheart!"

"Not that either!"

"I'll—"

His neighbor poked his head out. "Will you shut the fuck up? It's too goddamned early."

"Sorry," I said, nodding my head in apology.

"Assholes," the neighbor muttered, slamming the door.

Niki's head popped up the stairwell, mouth curved into a smirk. "Bye, Archer."

I lifted my hand, watched her disappear.

Only then did I go back into my apartment and close the door.

For the record, the woman made a hell of a cup of coffee.

CHAPTER TWELVE

Dominque, or apparently *Niki*

I WAS SMILING as I strode down the street, my walk of shame more like a walk of a hell of a good lay.

But the glow faded as I walked to my car a block away.

Because I'd spent the night.

What a singularly stupid thing to do.

Sighing, I turned the corner, Archer's apartment complex at my back. My car was just around the next bend, and—

I stopped.

Because the entire street was empty.

Or, at least, the side of the street where *I'd* parked was empty.

As in, my car was gone.

As in, *all* of the cars I'd parked around were gone. "What the fuck?" I whispered . . . and then my gaze caught on the sign overhead.

"*Fuck*," I breathed.

Street sweeping. This morning.

Fucking hell.

My car . . . had been towed?

I tilted my head back with a groan, staring up at the cloud-less, bright blue sky and tossing a mental curse its way. What right did it have to look so cheerful, so clear and sunny when my car had been towed?

This was what I got for not following my rules.

This was the result of my idiocy in staying the night.

I'd known better, but I'd wanted to spend more time with Archer because he was sexy and kind and because of the paint-ings, the expression on his face, the way he'd wrapped his robe around me, how he'd cleaned up while I'd made a mess of the sundaes.

So, I'd . . . been weak.

So . . . I'd wanted more.

And now my car had been towed.

That was karma or the universe smacking me back into place, reminding me that I couldn't have nice things—or nice men.

Because, for as dirty as Archer was in the bedroom, he was one of the nice ones.

And nice didn't work in my life.

Never had. Never would.

Sighing, I walked closer to the sign, squinting up at the number on the bottom, so I could call and figure out how to get my car back. I was just tapping it into my cell when I felt my skin prickle, and I spun.

"Whatcha doing, Niki baby?"

Heat and tingles, my stomach filled with butterflies—no, with *serpents*, writhing motherfuckers that both turned me on and made me feel nauseated as fuck.

My breathing stalled, and I was stupidly frozen in place, studying the slight red hint in the brown of Archer's hair. Then he smiled, soothing the vipers inside me like he was a snake charmer and my abdomen was the covered basket, its lid askew, the reptiles inside just waiting for him to play his flute.

"Going home," I muttered, pulling up the Lyft app.

"In what?"

"A car."

"*Your* car?"

Well, now, that was beside the point. Ignoring him, I strode down the street, trying to put some distance between us, but the infernal man followed me, keeping an easy pace beside me, even though I was taking as long of strides as I could manage.

"Did you want a ride?" A beat. "To wherever you're going."

I didn't even know where I was going.

It wasn't like I had loads of experience having my car towed. This was a once-in-a-lifetime thing for me.

"Streets look clean," he murmured, strolling next to me, casual as can be.

I stopped. Sighed.

"You know, I happen to be on a first-name basis with the impound lot owner," he said, still casual, but with enough humor in his tone that I was ready to rip out one of those fucking street sweeping signs and impale him with it.

"Why do I always think murderous thoughts when you're around?" I muttered.

A shrug. "I bring out the best in people."

I sniffed.

A grin. "It's a gift."

I kept walking, even though I had no reason to. I could call a Lyft from anywhere. But Archer didn't question me, just kept pace beside me, though I could feel his amusement in the air between us.

"I was serious about knowing Paulie."

Another sigh. "Who's Paulie?"

He snapped his fingers. "Keep up, Niki baby."

"Are you fucking kidding me?" I clipped out, shoving his hand away. "You're going to *snap* at me?"

"You're beautiful when you're angry. Did anyone ever tell you that?"

"Only the people who I cheerfully murdered." I stomped down the sidewalk.

His lips twitched . . . which I saw . . . because I couldn't keep my eyes off him for long, the motherfucker. "How many people is that?" he asked, picking up my hand and pressing a kiss to my palm.

I snatched it free. "One."

"Including or excluding me?"

I glared at him.

He just lifted a brow.

"Including," I admitted or rather, grumbled.

Laughter—his—and I tried to pretend it made me feel homicidal rather than amused, just the slightest bit. The fucker saw right through me, though he didn't say anything to give voice to that fact. Instead, it was . . . something I just knew in my soul. The same voice that had driven me to stay last night, that had kept me in bed when the coffee had worn off and my eyes had grown heavier, when I'd let Archer put on another movie, even though I'd felt sleep closing in on me.

He snagged my hand. "Come back to my place. I'll make you pancakes and call Paulie. Your car won't be back to the impound lot yet anyway."

I didn't immediately tug my fingers loose again, though I should have.

Instead, I left my hand in that warm clasp and asked, "How do you know that?"

That brow lifted again. "How do you think I know Paulie?" he asked. "When the parking lot at my apartment was being renovated, I had to park my car here more than a few times." He smiled. "And more than a few times, I forgot about the Tuesday/Thursday street-sweeping and didn't move my car in time." A shrug. "Which meant that I had to befriend Paulie."

"How many is more than a few?"

"More than a few," he said. "Fucker never gave me a break on fees, though."

I laughed then sighed and slowed to a stop. "How good are your pancakes?"

He grinned, full-on and cocky, and my pussy throbbed in memory. "As good as your sundaes."

And I knew I was so seriously fucked. I was going down. This was going to implode and go so, *so* bad.

But . . . I slid close to him.

If I was going down, I would at least embrace the ride.

Because I had the feeling it was going to be a hell of one.

"Pancakes," I said and turned to lead him back to his apartment.

CHAPTER THIRTEEN

Archer

I HADN'T MADE enough pancakes.

Not nearly enough, I realized when I turned back from the griddle to find the plate was nearly empty.

"What?" she asked, her mouth full when I stared at her agog.

"That was six pancakes," I said.

Six full-sized pancakes with chocolate chips and powdered sugar and syrup. The woman was going to be jittery from her sugar rush, or at least have a stomachache from the carbs alone.

"So?" she asked, the word muffled.

"So, that was supposed to be three each."

She froze, the last bite of pancake hanging off the edge of her fork. Then chewed, swallowed. "Then why'd you put them on one plate?"

"I was making it look pretty."

"Pretty?" She glanced at the table then back up at me, eyebrows arched. "But it's food."

I huffed, turned back to the bowl and started mixing more batter—a double batch this time.

"Where'd you learn to cook?"

I measured flour into the bowl, added eggs and milk, a dollop of oil, a teaspoon of baking soda. No chocolate chips, since I'd used the last of them for the first six pancakes, but that was okay. They'd still be good. After whisking the ingredients together, I ladled the batter onto the griddle. "My mom taught me," I said, watching the bubbles form on the back of the circles, growing and collecting until they covered the entire surface and popped, tiny craters telling me it was time to flip them.

I did so, aware of Niki coming closer, of her propping herself up on the counter as I turned each of the pancakes.

"What's your favorite thing?"

My gaze flicked to hers. "To cook?"

She nodded.

"*You're* asking *me* questions, now?"

A roll of deep brown eyes. "Yes, since it seems that I'm stuck with you, I might as well pull back the curtain."

The smallest tendril of hope curled through me. She could have called a car, could have told me to leave. Instead, she'd come back to my apartment and was asking me questions about myself.

"Pasta," I said, when I felt a shiver of impatience skate through her. "I have a family recipe for homemade spaghetti and Bolognese."

"Mmm." Her stomach rumbled, and I shook my head.

"How are you possibly hungry after six pancakes?"

"Don't judge me," she snapped. "I love food, and I love eating. Plus, my idea of pasta is opening a can and heating the slop in a microwave."

I dropped the spatula, and it bounced off the tile.

"Tell me you're kidding," I muttered, scooping the utensil up and tossing it into the sink, then opening another drawer to retrieve another turner before snagging the plate from the table.

"If I don't, will you make me that homemade pasta?"

"I'd make it for you either way."

She went still for a moment then scooped up one of the griddle-fresh pancakes from the plate and took a huge bite. "Mmm."

"It doesn't even have the syrup on it."

"I don't care," she said, the words almost indecipherable. "They're still delicious."

"Do you have a hollow leg?"

Her lips twitched. "You're not funny. I sometimes forget to eat when I'm working, so I make up for it when I'm not." She took another bite, chewed and swallowed. "Also, I really like food."

I liked the last.

I hated the first.

"Why don't you eat?"

A shrug. "I get carried away with my work, sometimes I glance up and the entire day has gone."

"I get that," I said, meaning it, knowing I'd done the same many times before.

She reached for another pancake as I ladled more batter then topped the ones on the plate with syrup and powdered sugar. As she ate the naked pancake, I retrieved the forks from the table and handed her hers. "I bet you do." Her eyes flicked to the studio with my shrine to all things Dominque then back to mine, amusement drifting across her face. "Go on and eat," she encouraged. "Before I scarf them down."

I pushed the plate toward her. "Yours."

I retrieved another from the cupboard. "Mine."

Mirth had her lips turning up. "Probably for the best," she said, scooping up a big bite. "What about painting, how'd you get into that?"

"I couldn't ever imagine doing anything else." I shrugged. "Luckily, I have some talent and an audience to buy them."

Her brows dragged together. "So, why are you working in the bar?"

"Kace needed help," I said, and when her brows didn't relax, I added the rest of the truth. "And I needed a fresh start after my divorce."

The fork was suspended an inch from her mouth. "Divorce?"

I nudged the tines closer. "Yup. I had the bad luck to both marry young and marry the wrong person."

"I'm sorry."

Since the pancakes were done, I flipped them on the plate then doused them liberally with sugar and syrup. "I'm not. It's been official for about six months now, but it was over long before that."

"Still sorry," she said before slipping the bite into her mouth.

"We wanted different things." I used the side of my fork to cut a chunk of pancakes. "Have you ever been serious with someone?" I asked, shoving the bite in while I waited to see if she would answer, if she'd give me something personal.

Brown eyes, deep pools of melted chocolate, met mine, hesitation in their depths. "Yes," she murmured.

Three letters.

What some might consider a minimal response.

And yet, those three letters gave me a wealth of information.

Yes, she'd loved someone.

Yes, they'd broken something in her.

Yes, I wanted to rip them limb from limb for daring to hurt her.

She pushed the plate away, half the second helping of pancakes consumed but now accompanying a sick expression, and I knew that as much as I wanted to know everything that had happened, to ferret out each bit of information about the asshole, she was getting ready to run.

Which meant I needed to switch gears.

"Have you always lived in the Bay Area?" I asked.

She swallowed, rolling the fork between thumb and forefinger. "No, I moved here about a year ago. More of my business was on this coast, and I didn't want to live in the city."

"I know the feeling," I said, thinking of this town we'd found ourselves in, just north of San Francisco, its peninsula approaching the Bay on one side and the ocean on the other, a quaint little downtown, low-slung buildings. There wasn't any structure over three stories, and the colorful houses blended in with the parks and green space to create a small town feel with many of the amenities of a big city.

"Where'd you live before?" she asked.

"LA."

"Hmm," she murmured, her head tilting to the side, her eyes on my face as she studied me like I was a slide under a microscope.

I put down my fork. "What?"

"You don't seem the LA type."

That much was true. I'd grown up on the central coast of California, spending my days on the beach, surfing in water that was colder than the beaches of SoCal, and my nights in the little farm town, drinking too much and finding trouble wherever I could.

And that trouble had been few and far between.

Because small town.

Because . . . truthfully, I wasn't much for trouble. Never had been. Never would be. Though, I thought, my gaze drifting to Dominque's, I was definitely into finding the type of trouble she'd bring. "Niki?" I murmured.

"Yeah?"

"I'm not the LA type." I grinned. "I could be *your* type, though."

She rolled her eyes. "You think you're charming."

"I *know* I'm charming," I teased, relaxing when she picked up her plate, went back to consuming large amounts of carbs.

"Shut up and eat," she muttered, shoving a bite in. "I need to get my car back."

———

"THAT'S EXTORTION," she grumbled as we walked out of the office. "Three hundred dollars?" Her scowl was fierce as she strode across the parking lot and handed her papers to the attendant.

I shrugged. "It's reality."

"It's a shitty reality," she huffed as she took back the papers and started walking in the direction the attendant pointed.

"That much is true," I said. "Next time, just park in my guest spot, Niki girl."

She glared at me. "First, what makes you think there's going to be a next time?" More glaring. "And second, why do you keep calling me Niki? No one in my life has ever called me—"

I snagged her hand, drew her against me. "Good," I said.

Fuck, she was pretty when she scowled. "That's ridiculous—"

I kissed her, sweet and spice in my nose, on my tongue, affection blossoming in my heart. Well, it had been there already, had been, to keep with the metaphor, blooming over the last month, and the extra time with her, with her sass and fierceness, had watered that vine, had helped it grow into something hearty, something with the promise of so much more.

"You taste like pancakes," I murmured, after gentling the kiss, after slowly peeling my lips from hers.

My hand was still in her hair, the silken locks beyond soft, matching the emotion in her eyes, and I had the sense that I'd won a victory, albeit a small one. She smiled. "What else can you cook?"

"Park in my guest spot tonight and find out," I cajoled.

"I . . . can't."

That sense of victory tanked, the promise shriveling up. I still had plenty of determination, wouldn't give up easily, not when whatever this connection between us was more than just lust. But I could also only do so much in pursuit. If she truly didn't want me, want more between us, then it wasn't like I could force her to like me enough to take the leap.

Either she would jump, or she wouldn't.

However, that didn't mean I wouldn't attempt to charm her into taking that first step and—

"I have to work," she said, and I didn't think I was losing it when I thought I saw real regret in her expression. "And it'll be late, considering that I've spent the morning downing pancakes when I should be searching through servers and organizing data." She stepped back, and I released her hair.

"You're sexy when you talk about your work."

She bleeped her key fob, and I heard her car respond the next row over. "Should I discuss security parameters? Or maybe tell you how to avoid ransomware?" She smiled. "I can also give you techniques for how to utilize the back door."

My cock twitched.

It shouldn't have, since I wasn't into anal.

But . . . I think I'd be into pretty much anything if it involved this woman. Role playing, spanking, toys, public sex. The only limiting factor would be my imagination—and I had a vivid fucking imagination.

"You know, you never told me why you call me Niki."

I hadn't.

Because I didn't have a good reason.

To me, she was just . . . Niki. And that no one else called her that was a bonus. It was another thread between us, tying us together, tying *her* to me when I was desperate to keep growing those connections.

"You hate it?" I asked.

Dominque paused, her hand on the door handle. "No." A sigh. "I just . . . well, my childhood wasn't one for informalities. My parents were strict, and I don't just mean about using my full name."

I leaned against the roof of her car. "What else were they strict about?"

She was quiet for so long I expected her to not answer, especially when she tugged open the driver's side door and sat down in the seat. "An easier question to answer would be what *weren't* they strict about?"

"Boys?" I asked lightly.

Laughter. "Yes, they were strict about *boys*."

"And clothes?"

A roll of her eyes. "Yes, also about clothes."

"Movies? TV shows?"

"What, is this a rundown of the typical teenage girl's life?"

"No," I teased, crouching down next to the car, resting my palm on her thigh. "It's a rundown of *my* life."

She had a magnificent smile, one that seemed to change the atmosphere around her, making it writhe and tingle with electricity. Static crawling down the skin on my bare arms, lifting the hairs there, that charge gathering, waiting, just coiling, readying itself to release.

"Such a wild thing," she said sardonically.

"So true," I told her. "Give me an easel and paints, and I just go bananas."

More smiling, though this one was accompanied by laughter that glazed over all the rough spots inside me, smoothing out the barbed edges, so that when she asked, "What were your parents like?"

"Great," I said, the memories washing over me. Fuck, they'd been really great, had filled my life with easy happiness. I'd never for a moment wondered if I'd been loved. "I was one of the lucky ones. My friends would always hang at my house because they were so cool."

"Let me guess"—her lips curved—"your mom would bake homemade cookies and deliver them to you and your friends while you juggled game controllers."

"Not quite," I said, squeezing her leg. "My dad would make the cookies. My mom was a doctor with her own practice. My dad stayed home with me and my brother."

Her eyes were soft. "Where do they live now?"

I froze, the warm memories of youth erased by the cold reality of adulthood. "They died a couple of years ago in a sailing accident."

Her face changed, growing sad, and I hated that my truth had caused that. "Archer," she murmured.

"It's okay. My brother is still in LA, and we have each other."

She inhaled, released it slowly, covering my hand with hers. "I'm glad you two have each other."

"Thanks, sweetheart."

Her thumb brushed over the back of my hand, sending tingles up my arm, warmth toward my heart. "What about your parents?"

"Alive and in Ohio." She shook her head. "Still spreading plenty of disapproval my way."

I squeezed her thigh again. "Siblings?"

"Nope." The P sounded like a *pop*, her smile not the lovely one from moments before. "Just me to shatter all their dreams."

"Dominque," I began.

"No." She shifted, turned to face me, expression drawn. "I'm Niki to you, remember? I'm not her, not Dominque. Let me be Niki instead—in-instead of—"

Her gaze dropped, but not before I saw the yearning, the glistening of tears in her eyes. The pain and the regret creating grooves by that lush mouth.

"Okay, baby," I said, nodding. "Okay, Niki. It's okay."

She slipped her hand from beneath mine, wiped her eye. "This is your fault," she muttered.

"Yes," I agreed.

"I'm in a parking lot after my car was towed, crying over stuff that will never change, stuff that is ancient history." She sniffed then nudged my hand off her thigh. "Anyway, it doesn't matter, does it?"

"It matters," I said. "*You* matter."

Still. Her body went statue still then she shook her head, smiled gently. "Had to be a fucking charmer, didn't you?"

I brushed my finger over her bottom lip. "It's a gift."

"Ack." She shoved me back lightly. "I've got to work."

Finding my feet, I asked, "Tomorrow?"

Her brows dragged together, and she gripped the steering wheel, and I thought for sure she would say no. Then she extended a hand. "Give it."

Now I frowned. "Give what?"

"Your cell. If I'm going to use that guest parking spot, you need my number, so you can tell me where it is."

I handed it over.

She plugged her number in but then held it out of reach. "Homemade pasta and Bolognese?"

"If you commit to the night after, I'll even make a cheesecake."

She moaned.

My cock twitched.

Then her chocolate eyes came to mine. "You've got a deal." She plunked my cell into my hand, nudged me back a little farther, and reached for the door.

I caught it, bent, wedging it open with my hip.

"What now?" she snapped, though her amusement was tangible.

"This." I kissed her, long and slow and deep, swallowing her moans, giving her back mine, along with my heart. Though, I supposed that had happened the moment she'd glared up at me at the bar. Eventually, though, I had to release her, had to let her get on with her day. "Tomorrow," I promised. "And I'll text you tonight."

"I might not answer."

I cupped her cheek. "Then I'll just text you again. Okay?"

A long moment of quiet, her eyes studying mine, emotions flickering across her expression too quickly for me to decipher, and for a moment, I thought she was going to take everything back, to call an end to this, before we really got going.

Then I saw a thread of determination drift through her chocolate gaze, and my lungs began working again.

"Okay," she murmured.

CHAPTER FOURTEEN

Niki

THE TEXT HAPPENED, just as he'd promised.

The *second* text.

Since I'd purposely ignored the first text.

But that second *buzz-buzz* one hour and twelve minutes after the first—not that I was counting or anything—had me releasing my mouse and picking up my cell.

The first text had been:

Since I know you're going to ignore this . . .

And that was it.

Just ". . ." and leaving me on the hook for the second half of the sentence while I counted, didn't count? Did? I sighed. Okay, *had* counted. I'd gotten markedly little work done because I'd been clocking the minutes passing on that tiny clock in the upper right side of my computer.

Which meant I'd spent the last hour and twelve minutes being absolutely useless.

I quickly unlocked the screen, not wanting to see the

preview, wanting to actually click on that green icon with the red bubble at its corner.

Because . . .

Why?

I didn't even know. I didn't understand why I'd stayed last night, why I felt this unrelenting urge to spend time with Archer, why I'd stayed that morning, why I was anticipating his text so much, even now.

I was a buoy in the ocean.

Alone, bobbing up and down, not lonely because I spent my life doing my job, and even though it was a job that most people probably didn't think of, it was still one that was important.

Predicting tsunamis.

Taking down bad guys.

Equal importance, right?

Shaking my head at my idiocy, I decided that I was going to focus less on the why, less on the inevitable end. Instead, I was going to live right now, right in this moment.

Probably stupid.

But . . . I'd spent a lot of my life being smart. I could take some time to be stupid, especially when it involved a man like Archer.

And also, I was tired of being that isolated buoy. I was tired of being alone and distant. I wanted . . . well, perhaps it was time I moved beyond my rules, that I took down the barbed wire. Because . . .

Archer was pretty fucking great.

Even if I still had the niggling in the back of my mind, my parents' voices and my self-doubt in the collective, telling me it was inevitable that I'd fuck this up.

Maybe—

My cell buzzed again, reminding me I hadn't read the message.

Which meant it was time to look at the text.

I clicked the green box, tapped his message chain . . .

Burst out laughing.

And you'll probably ignore this . . .

"Fucker," I muttered, my fingers flying across the screen.

I happened to say I'd only ignore the first text.

A moment later my phone vibrated again.

No, you said you'd probably ignore me. I said I'd text again.

I thought back, realized that—shit—he was right.

I will neither confirm nor deny.

He was probably laughing his ass off right now.

Also, my texting strategy was successful since you're texting back.

Also right, the fucker. Which had me lying.

I was done with work.

Because I clearly hadn't finished what I needed to when I was a tangle of anticipation.

The ". . ." appeared then disappeared. Then reappeared again. *Then* disappeared again.

And finally, when I was getting so exasperated that I was ready to launch my phone out the window, it rang.

Who talked on the phone nowadays?

That was just . . .

It stopped ringing.

Another message buzzed through.

Do I need to come to your front porch again? Pick up the call,
Niki baby.

I shouldn't. More conversation would breed more connection . . . but I'd already promised to go to his apartment the next day, and then again for another time. It would be silly not to talk to him now when I'd said I would be going to his place for two more dates—

Not dates.

Um . . . mutual satisfactory happy time . . . with orgasms thrown in.

That didn't sound delusional, right?

Not. At. All.

My cell rang again, and living in that delusion, I swiped my finger across the screen and lifted it to my ear.

"Was it the *baby* that got you to pick up?"

I sighed, leaned back in my very expensive office chair. It was technically a gaming chair with amazeballs lumbar support and enough adjustability that my short ass legs could reach the floor and my T-Rex arms could touch my keyboard.

"The Niki then," he said when I didn't speak. "I can't say I hate that I'm the one with the special nickname for you."

"It's all that possessive maleness."

"You say that like it's a disease."

My brows lifted, not that he could see them. "Isn't it?"

He paused. "I suppose it is."

My laughter bubbled up like champagne threatening to escape from the top of the bottle. And it *did* escape, a silly-sounding giggle that had me cringing and sobering. "What are we doing, Archer?" I asked. "I have rules, but you and your dumb cock have me breaking them."

Except, even as I said that, I knew it was more than the sex.

It was just . . . Archer.

He made me wonder about possibilities and consider if

perhaps my rules were less about protecting me and more about . . . hiding. Fuck. Was I hiding?

The silence stretched before he spoke. "I like you," he said. "For me, it's as simple as that. I saw you across the bar, glaring at me, deliberately ignoring me, and I had to know you."

"So you're saying I was a challenge."

"*Was?*"

"Ugh." I pushed my chair back, the wheels squeaking against the floor. "You're just trying to be annoying."

"You are rather pretty when you're annoyed."

"But not at other times?" I asked, my tone deadly.

A beat. "Nope."

I laughed, despite myself, pushing out of my chair and heading down the hall to the stairs. I was finished pretending to work for the night. I'd gotten enough done that I wouldn't be critically behind the next day, and clearly, staring at my phone for over an hour hadn't done me any favors. I might as well stop spinning my wheels and just really get back on it tomorrow. Plus, I was hungry. I was tired. I wanted some of my canned pasta and a glass of wine.

The perfect pairing.

"I know I shouldn't encourage you," I said, strolling into the kitchen and opening the pantry. "But—"

"I'm infinitely charming?"

"But you're occasionally amusing, so I don't mind keeping you around," I said, making my tone joking, even though what I'd said felt a bit like the truth. Scarily so. And for a moment, loathing filled me, hating that I was scared of something as good and pure as Archer. I was supposed to be fearless. I'd left my life behind. I'd rebuilt this new one in my image.

I wasn't supposed to be scared of a single fucking thing.

But I was.

Fucking hell. Pushing the slicing disgust down, I reached up to grab my favorite can of pasta—tiny raviolis filled with something that was supposedly cheese, although I wasn't entirely convinced of that fact.

"I'll take occasionally amusing," he said then paused, and I could practically hear the gears of his brain working through my speaker. "What are you doing?"

I dipped my finger into the cold contents, scooped up some of the yumminess. "Eating," I said between bites.

Yes, I was eating it cold.

Yes, I was really hungry.

Yes, I had questionable nutrition habits.

But *c'est la vie* and all that.

I hadn't eaten since the pancakes that morning, and I was wasting away. Pretty soon my hollow leg would grow, would consume my torso, my arms.

Ha.

If only that were true.

"Eating what?" Archer asked, suspicion evident.

"You don't want to know," I said, retrieving a spoon from the drawer because I could only be undignified for so long. *Heh.* Mostly, it was because my spoon was simply a better utensil for shoving my tiny raviolis into my mouth. My stomach rumbling, I returned to the pantry and grabbed another can. I'd eat this one cold while I waited for the other to heat in the microwave.

Well, I'd dump it into a bowl first. I couldn't risk blowing up the single appliance I used.

"*Niki*," he warned.

"Not gonna tell you." Though, of course, it sounded a lot like, "Snof donna shmell to."

Apparently, Archer could speak Dominque—or rather, Niki baby, I thought with a smile—because he said, "Put the can down and step toward your front door."

Brows drawing together, I spun in a circle, half-convinced he'd somehow made his way into my house and could see me noshing on my baby raviolis. But, dumbshit, if he were inside, I would have heard him talking, especially if he were near enough that he could see me playing raccoon while I tried to scrape every last bit out of my can.

"What are you talking about?"

"I know your bloodstream is probably currently overrun with salt after your processed food foray," he said, teasing, making his tone roll through the air, along my eardrums, and into my brain.

Or maybe my heart.

Both were terrifying.

One perhaps slightly more. I just didn't know which . . . okay, I *did* know. I just wasn't ready to admit it yet.

Especially when it was my heart.

Gah!

Enough.

"Niki?"

"What?" I asked, licking the back of my spoon.

"Put the can down. And go open your front door."

I finally processed what he was saying and what it might mean. "Are you here?" I asked, experiencing a strange buoyancy I didn't want to explore too closely.

"No."

Pop.

Deflated, I tried to temper my tone. "Oh."

"But I'll be there in . . ." I heard a soft *click*, a sudden quiet, as though the background noise had cut out. As though he'd just parked and turned off his car. ". . . thirty seconds."

"Thirty—?" I dropped the can into the trash, the spoon into the sink, along with a couple of plates and cups I hadn't gotten around to washing the day before. Luckily, my consumption of processed food—cough, out of the cans themselves—meant that I didn't have a lot of dishes. But I wasn't the cleanest person, and Archer was a neat freak. And—

Oh, God. What was I wearing?

I nearly dropped my phone as I tried to look down at my clothes, at my "hacking" outfit, which basically consisted of a tank top along with the oldest, ugliest, *holiest* pair of sweats I owned, a giant, half-bleached hoodie—half because during my last cleaning phase I'd had a misfire while trying to scrub my toilet—along with no bra, no underwear, and giant fluffy pink socks.

I was a blob of gray with strange pink tentacles and—

Knock-knock.

"Fuck," I breathed.

"Niki."

I didn't answer him, just kept the phone to my ear as I did one of those weird-ass flurry of movements I'd seen heroines in romantic comedies do—flying around the room, ripping off the sweatshirt and running to the laundry room. And then fighting with the laundry room door, since there was a dirty load sitting on the floor just on the other side of it that I'd been meaning to take care of . . . along with a clean one sitting in a basket on the dryer.

Clean clothes.

Small victories.

"Niki," Archer said again, the knock coming a second time.

I put the cell on speaker, tossed it on the washer. "Just a second!"

One jerk to toss the sweatshirt on the pile, leaving me in just my tank top. Another to drop my pants alongside it. I didn't have time to search for underwear or a bra, just grabbed the first bottoms that my hands rested on—black leggings thankfully—and then ran out of the laundry room, wrestling with the door again on my way out.

I paused—actually paused—to study my hair in the reflection of the fridge (seriously, what the *fuck?*) before I remembered myself and ran to the door.

Knock—

I yanked it open.

And sweet baby Jesus, what right did the man have to look so fucking gorgeous? Huh? *Huh?*

Especially when he just held up a bag, one that smelled wonderful, and asked, "Hungry?"

"Fuck you!" I slammed the door, banged my head against it.

The man was too fucking wonderful, and I was feeling way too insecure and as though I never could measure up. I had intentionally ignored his first text, been snarky on the call, and meanwhile, he had been on the way to my place with food that smelled even better than my tiny raviolis, *and* he didn't seem to care that I'd just shut the door in his face.

As though the man had X-ray vision, his next knock came right against my forehead, his voice carrying laughter as it drifted through the wood. "Should I just leave this right here then?"

I groaned, reached for the doorhandle and tugged it open. Again.

"Where's your cell?" he asked.

My sigh was heavy, lifting and dropping my shoulders on an inhale and exhale. My phone was still in the laundry room, sitting on top of the washer, probably still connected to Archer's in all my speakerphone glory, considering he still held his in one hand.

"Why are you here?" I groaned.

"I can go."

I groaned again. "No, Archer. I just . . . fuck, I'm a pain in the ass, and you're here anyway and—"

"You, Niki. I just like you. That's it." He stroked a hand down my arm, making me shiver, making me shift closer. "There isn't an ulterior motive, except"—a curve of his lips —"that if I keep feeding you, maybe you'll let me hang out for a while longer."

Hope was a roiling thing inside me. It should feel good, this new glow of meeting someone, of liking him, of wanting nothing more than to spend time with him. But it didn't feel good, or at least not *only* good because of the giant elephant sitting on my chest, the irrefutable choice. My lips parted and I blurted, "I'm going to disappoint you. I *always* disappoint people who try to care about me."

Archer was statue still, his face a study in shock. But almost as I processed that, the shock disappeared, pushed out by fury that turned down his mouth, that shot sparks through his hazel eyes. He pushed past me, slamming the door behind him, throwing the lock, setting the bag of food on the table I kept in the hall for my keys and other shit that I didn't feel like carrying any farther than the front hall.

Then he turned back to me, and the ferocity of his expression had me skittering back a step.

And another.

But then he was there, right in front of me, forcing me into a farther retreat, forcing me down the hall until my back was against the wall, until his front was firmly pressed to mine, his hands on either side of my head, closing in on me, creating a bubble of just him and me, a tiny world that only existed for us.

He crouched down, blazing hazel eyes locking with mine. "You don't see yourself."

That hadn't been what I expected him to say, not with the fury in his expression. I'd braced for a lash of words, waiting for them to permeate my skin, to activate that spike inside me, to have it fly forward and eviscerate me.

Instead, he just stayed in place, still as that statement washed over me.

And it did.

A warm shower after being trapped in the freezing rain, soaking into my hair, trailing down my nape, my arms, my back, warming me, pushing the chill away.

"I see," he said at the same time that heat had reached my fingertips, "a woman who's smart and a hard worker. Who's talented and strong and sexy as hell. Who knows what she wants but doesn't see the magic inside."

If he'd led with *the magic inside*, I probably would have burst out laughing, would have been able to discount the rest of it easily.

But he'd begun with the other stuff.

The ones that were more difficult to disregard.

I was smart. I *did* work hard. I was strong. Though, talented was borderline—I'd just developed the skills I'd needed for this career, so I supposed in some way, that *was* true. As for sexy . . . well, I didn't shy away from sex in normal times. I'd never felt insecure about my body. And while it wasn't like I was out parading through Bone Town every night, I didn't exactly shy away from getting orgasms when the opportunity presented itself.

Case in point, Archer.

But . . . I didn't feel like I had magic inside.

I was just . . . me, a woman who was better alone because no matter how hard I tried, there would always be a tipping point in every relationship.

And it would tip *away* from me, dropping me down into a pit of emptiness.

Which, look, I got sounded very dramatic. But it was true. I'd tried. *Oh,* how I'd tried. First with my parents. Then with any boy I could get to date me, who expressed interest in me. I'd spent loads of time changing myself, trying to fit into different molds. For years, I'd done that. Right up until . . .

"I left my fiancé at the altar."

He blinked, probably rightly wondering how in the fuck-all he'd gone from telling me I had *magic* to me describing the time I played runaway bride.

"That was the last straw for my parents," I said. "They were furious that they'd paid for a wedding to a man, who was 'perfect in every way,' only to have me literally running out of the church minutes before the ceremony went down."

Archer didn't move, his chest just calmly rising and falling against mine. "What made you run?"

Funny.

No one had ever asked me that question. Not really. I'd gotten, "How could you do that to Derek?" and, "How dare you leave?" and my personal, painful favorite accompanied by my mom's furious, whip-sharp tone, "Why would you do that? Why would you do that to *me?*"

Derek's questions, rightly, had been along the vein of, "Why did you leave me?" and, "God, why *then?*"

But no one had ever cared enough to truly understand what had propelled me to run down the street in my wedding dress, heart pounding, palms sweaty, hating that I was hurting people but knowing that I couldn't, *couldn't* stay.

And by the time I'd understood enough *to* explain why I *hadn't* been able to stay, it had been too late.

Derek had gotten married. To a bride who'd stayed.

He'd cut off all contact with me. My parents and friends had done the same. I was the pariah who made things complicated in our social circle.

Which had been fine.

I'd hated the person I'd let those societal pressures become. Outside of it, I'd allowed myself to grow, become different. Find this job, start my business, disappoint several other good men along the way.

"I ran because I couldn't find myself anymore."

His brows drew together, and I expected him to frown, to pull back, for that explanation to make no sense.

Instead, he said, "I know just what you mean."

And that unhitched me, freed my lungs, unclenched my hands.

Making me . . . think that maybe . . . maybe I wouldn't actually fuck this up.

Maybe with Archer, everything could be different. That perhaps I could be me, *just* me, and that wouldn't be a disappointment.

He laced our fingers together, picked up the bag of food from the table, and led me back down the hall, peeking through openings until he'd found the kitchen. A nudge to get me in a chair, more peeking to find plates and utensils, and then he'd scooped up something that wasn't homemade Bolognese, but some sort of creamy chicken and rice combo, onto two plates.

One of which he placed in front of me.

The other next to me, where he took a seat.

"How?" I asked, even though it wasn't really any of my business, especially since I wasn't exactly an open book. "How do you know what I mean?"

His eyes drifted to mine, a thread of gentleness that probably should have pissed me off, that definitely should have made me push him away. And in the past, it would have. But today, with *him*, with this buoyant feeling in my chest, I did neither.

Instead, that gentle tone had me melting slowly from top to bottom or maybe bottom to top, or maybe both—an ice cube on the sidewalk, the heat of the concrete defrosting me at an equal pace to that of the sun. The tender was the sun. The lack of artifice in his response was the sidewalk. The way he set down his fork and reached up to tuck a strand of hair behind my ear was . . . I don't know. The microwave or a magnifying glass or a . . .

Something hot that melted me from the inside out.

Go me.

So words weren't exactly my strong suit. But I was trying here. I wasn't running screaming, even despite the big feelings. I was waiting to continue an emotional conversation with a man who terrified me because I wanted more than just a quick fuck.

If that wasn't growth, I didn't know what was.

Archer's fingers shook slightly as he brushed them over my cheek, as he closed them into a fist that he then rested on his thigh. "After my parents died, I wasn't myself. I was engaged to my ex, and we'd already planned the wedding." He sighed, stroked his thumb over my palm. "I'd known things weren't right for a while, but we'd been together for so long that I didn't know how to stop the ball from rolling. It was like I was strapped into the roller coaster and not in the least bit ready for the ride, but . . . I didn't get off. I just let the operator push the button to send us off, and it was too late."

"And it went wrong," I said carefully when he didn't say anything further.

"Yeah, or stayed wrong or . . . we just didn't want the same things anymore," he said, his eyes unfocused, telling me he was in that past, lost in those memories. "I think if we'd started dating as adults, we never would have gotten married." He blew out a breath. "I think if my parents had been alive, I wouldn't have gone through with it at all."

"I'm sorry," I whispered.

A shrug. "We're better off apart. She's remarried and happy. I'm able to live how I like, able to build my life around people who aren't always looking at our relationship as something where we have to keep score."

"My parents were like that," I whispered, the admission coming without thought.

It was just that he'd shared, that he'd opened up, and I felt like I owed him the same.

No, not *owed*.

I *wanted* to share, wanted this man to know me. Not because of some scoreboard, but because I wanted to get close to him. I wanted to let him in. And maybe that was critically stupid considering my past experiences with men, with my parents.

But . . . Archer.

With him, I couldn't bar the door, couldn't continue to keep the gates closed. He'd battered them down. *No.* He had the key because I wanted him close, had hope that he wouldn't look closely, see what was inside me, and find me lacking.

And if he did?

My heart spasmed.

Well, the ride would hopefully be worth it.

"Everything was transactional," I said, when he just continued to stroke my palm with his thumb, waiting patiently for me to get my mind wrapped around my thoughts. "I did what they wanted—exactly what they wanted—and things were great. I had all the toys, the video games, the treats I wanted. If I spoke out of turn or questioned something or, heaven forbid, made my own decision, then it was like I murdered someone's cat."

I tugged my hand free, pushed out of my chair, and paced back and forth across the kitchen. "God, the punishments for not wearing a certain blouse or for asking to have a certain meal." I stopped, spun back. "I'm not saying I was the perfect kid. I had my temper tantrums. I definitely deserved some of the punishments . . ."

"But," Archer murmured when I let that trail off for a long while, "not all of them."

"No," I agreed. "But I lived that way for a long time. I dated who they said to date. I studied what they said to study. And I was going to marry who they said to marry." Fucking hell, I'd dodged a bullet there. If I'd walked down that aisle, I would have continued to live a small life, boxed in and compressed from all directions, not thinking for myself, not living for myself. "I was weak for a long time," I said, "but eventually, I couldn't take it anymore."

"What happened?"

The memories washed over me, a cold wave sneaking up and out of the Pacific, snatching me and dragging me into the frigid sea. "I exploded. I called off the wedding . . . or rather, I ran away from it. In my dress and heels, my veil flying behind me. The perfectly done makeup and hair. I finally saw what was waiting for me at the end of the aisle, and I just couldn't do it."

"What'd you do then?"

"I ran all the way home, if you can believe it." God, my feet had hurt. I'd kicked off my heels, ran with bare feet until I'd made it home. "And then I changed. Packed a suitcase, bought a bus ticket to California, and I moved on with my life."

My parents had been absolutely furious.

I'd tried to call them from the road, wanting to let them know I was okay. And after my parents were sure I wasn't coming home, wasn't going to beg Derek for forgiveness, to go through with the wedding, they disowned me completely.

Probably for the best.

If I'd stayed, my life wouldn't have been this big. I would have been limited, too afraid to step outside the box and go for the things I wanted because . . .

I froze, felt my face go pale. My heart pounded against my ribs, a cold sweat slicking down my spine when I realized—

"What is it, sweetheart?"

"Hold on," I said, breathing heavily as I sank down into a crouch, my fingers burying themselves into my hair. "I'm having an existential crisis here."

Fucking hell.

Because I realized that I'd made myself small anyway.

I'd left that life to find something more, to live loud and big and . . .

I hadn't.

I hadn't gone for relationships I'd wanted because I was scared and weak. I'd let go and burrowed deep into my safe shelter of work, of distance, of being disconnected. And I'd let stuff fly by me, drift away into the atmosphere, able to accept it because I'd convinced myself that it wouldn't have worked out anyway.

I'd left to find myself, to live big and full and instead . . . I hadn't.

This time *I* was the one who'd made myself small.

I was so *fucking* stupid.

CHAPTER FIFTEEN

Archer

ONE SECOND, she'd looked absolutely distraught, crouched on the floor, her hands in her hair.

I'd gotten up, crossed to her, concerned by the expression on her face.

And the next instant, she'd launched herself at me, knocking me back onto my ass, causing us both to sprawl across the floor.

"Oh, shit," she said, patting at my chest. "I'm sorry. I just—"

"First, don't apologize for climbing on top of me." I waggled my brows then grinned when she rolled her eyes. "Second"—I cupped her cheek—"what was that about an existential crisis?"

Her face shadowed, anger flashing across her face.

Then she sighed, and it melted away. "I left home to live my own life, but I fucking brought that small, stifling existence with me. I made it impossible to ever consider that I wouldn't disappoint friends or partners. I didn't even give myself the chance to figure out what *I* wanted." Tears in those brown eyes. "I gave up. I failed."

"That's bullshit," I said. A trickle of hurt crept into the lines of her mouth, and I quickly added, "I didn't mean it like that. I just . . . you figured out work. I only know whatever glossed-over version you can tell people about your job, but I know it's big and important and that you're really good at it." I ran my finger over her bottom lip when she opened her mouth to protest. "I'm not saying you're not right about the personal stuff, just that when you're saying you failed, you didn't."

"I've run from any shred of intimacy since the moment I left home."

I slid my hand from her cheek down to the side of her neck. "And I married someone I knew I shouldn't have, just because my parents died."

Her eyes flashed. "You had trauma."

I lightly squeezed her neck. "*So did you.*"

Niki inhaled sharply.

"The past doesn't define the path we choose now. You can be different. You don't have to fit into the mold your parents created, or even the one *you* created." I gently gripped her neck again. "Today, you can change. Today, you can take one step in the direction of the person you want to be."

Her breath shuddered out. "How?"

"How what?" I asked. I'd thrown a lot at her in the last few statements.

Eyes sliding closed, her body shifting forward on mine, bending until she rested her forehead on my collarbone. "How can you be so smart and well-adjusted?"

I laughed. "Most of the time, I feel the opposite." Threading my fingers into her hair, I lifted her head so I could meet her eyes. "But truthfully, I know I'm a work in progress, and after my parents died, I was really messed up. I pushed through to the wedding, I think half just on adrenaline and half because it was already planned. But a week after my honeymoon, I crashed. I couldn't get out of bed, was depressed. For months, I just shrank into a shell of myself." I shook my head. "Eventually, though, my baby brother hauled me to therapy, helped me get the medication I needed, and sat in the waiting room for me twice a week while I got my head straight. My *baby* brother looked after me."

"He loves you."

A nod. "The therapy helped. It took a long time to work through everything, to come to terms with the loss, with my failure to live on in some meaningful way when my parents had lost the chance to do the same, the added guilt that came from not being the strong one." My heart throbbed at the memory, at the agony of my parents being gone, at the pain of realizing that everything in my life had changed in one moment. "Eventually, I was able to wean off the medication, to get back to my art, to start living again, and . . . to realize that my marriage wasn't working."

She inhaled. "So, you came up here?"

"Kace reached out, asked if I could do him a solid, and my divorce was just final. A move made sense. I needed a fresh start, and it wasn't too far from my brother." I ran my fingers through her hair. "Then some woman glared at me from across the bar a month ago, and it was like everything inside me had realigned, refocused, and I finally felt alive again."

"Archer," she murmured.

"Still hate my name?" I teased lightly.

A light swat, though her eyes danced. "It is a terrible name," she said, "but since it's the name of the man I'm dating, then I guess I just have to deal with it."

"Dating?" I asked.

She nodded. "Dating." A beat, a slender thread of insecurity weaving through her expression. "Unless—"

I pistoned up, slanting my mouth across hers, kissing her with every bit of emotion I felt—affection and warmth, fury that she'd been so hurt, understanding that the past had brought us both together, and desire . . . the raging need this woman stoked inside me.

"Eat," I burst out, setting her away from me. "The food is getting cold."

Niki froze, her brown eyes wild, her hair an absolute mess from my fingers, her lips swollen and tempting me to taste her again. Then she blinked and laughed, standing up and offering her hand. "Let's eat."

———

THE CLICK-CLICKING WOKE ME UP, and it took a minute for me to process the sound.

Then I peeled back my lids, saw the rectangle of faint blue light shining under the closed door to the right.

I'd slept in Niki's bed.

After I'd eaten in Niki's kitchen.

After she'd shared . . .

So much. After *I'd* shared. After she hadn't kicked me out the front door, running from the moment of intimacy.

So yeah, that hope, the thin vine that had been growing over the last few days had been fertilized, for lack of a better term, and was now hearty, its roots gripping tight beneath the surface.

But now the bed was empty, the *click-clicking* coming through the door the only sign of the sexy, curvy woman.

I slipped out from beneath the covers, padded across the carpet to find my boxer briefs—tossed there by a torture-minded Niki some number of hours before. Not that I'd minded the torture of her kissing every inch of my body. It was the sweetest temptation, the best torment I'd ever undergone, especially when she'd allowed me to give her the same treatment in return.

Stepping into the boxers, I tried to gauge what time it was. She had blackout shades on her windows, so I couldn't tell if we'd slept the entire night, or if it had just been a few hours. I wasn't exhausted, so maybe more than a few. Although, I definitely had more energy when I was around her.

As though just being in her presence brightened my life.

And I supposed that was how it should be.

Not bereft without her there. Not weighed down when with her. But also just . . . *more* when I was near her.

Maybe that didn't make any sense.

Maybe I was beyond caring if it did or not.

I approached the door and knocked softly, not wanting to interrupt if she was busy, but the door must not have been shut all the way because the moment my fist made contact with the wood, it slid open to reveal . . .

A pants-less Niki standing at her computer, wearing just a tiny pair of underwear and a loose tank top.

No bra.

Which I knew because when she turned toward me, the light from the monitors shone right through that thin material.

Breasts.

Sweet Christ, she had a magnificent set.

"You're staring," she murmured.

"You're gorgeous," I countered.

Her lips curved, but then her computer chimed, and she glanced back at the screen, cursing as she bent closer, her fingers flying over the keyboard. "No, no," she moaned, tilting another screen toward her, images appearing and disappearing faster than I could track. "Shit," she muttered. "Fucking, motherfucker." Somehow, her fingers flew faster, and I slipped out of the room, closing the door behind me before making my way over to my pants, digging in my pocket until I found my cell.

Seven-thirty-two.

She'd let me stay the whole night, hadn't booted me out or run away, though I supposed the latter would have been challenging, considering it was *her* house. Still, before the issue with her work, she'd smiled at me.

So, I was taking seven-thirty-two as a victory.

I tugged on my pants, my shirt, tracked down my shoes and socks before moving quietly out of the bedroom and downstairs, where I surveyed the meager contents of Niki's fridge and pantry (dismal) and decided to brew some coffee before heading down the street toward the bakery I'd spotted when driving over.

While the pot hissed and spit, I took care of the dishes in the sink—something that Niki wouldn't let me touch the night before and something I couldn't ignore this morning. Especially, since it only took a few minutes.

Then when the coffee was done, I poured a cup, brought it upstairs, and swapped it out with an empty mug on her desk, even as she continued typing. She didn't glance away from the screen, nor even acknowledge me, but I didn't get my feelings hurt. I knew something of what it was like to be so focused on my work that the rest of the world faded away, and if something was going wrong, I wasn't going to mess with her flow.

I closed the door behind me, stumbled upon a spare set of keys as I headed outside, locked up, and made my way down the street.

The bakery, less than a block away, had a small storefront, but through the glass on the swinging double doors, I could see a large industrial kitchen with several workers buzzing around.

When the bell overhead rang as I entered, a blonde with blue-green eyes appeared, wiping her hands on her apron that was emblazoned with . . .

"Iris?" I asked.

She smiled, came over, and gave me a hug. "Archer, it's good to see you." She was married to Brent, the former full-time bartender turned student-slash-now-very-rare-fill-in at Bobby's. "It's been ages."

I'd taken Brent's position in the afternoon/evenings when he'd gotten too busy with school, and I was well-familiar with her delicious baked goods. "I didn't know you owned this place," I said. The last I'd heard, she had a small kitchen near the bar.

"We moved a couple of months ago." A shrug. "Outgrew the

last space." Her head tilted to the side. "I didn't think you lived in this part of town."

"I . . ." Here, I faltered, wondering what Niki would think about me sharing a piece of information that would surely get back to the bar, and thus, back to her employee, Hayden. But she'd told me we were dating, and people who were dating didn't hide. Not unless it was some romance novel or romcom fake relationship thing, and since this was neither of those two things, I said, "I'm actually dating Dominque, so I wanted to come in and pick up some treats for her."

Mention the dating.

Mention the baked goods.

Keep my nickname to myself.

"*Hayden's* Dominque?" Iris asked, raising her brows.

I nodded.

Iris smiled. "Oh, that's perfect! I actually just pulled out her favorite from the oven." She walked back behind the counter, pulled a pink box from somewhere and began folding it up. "I'll go package up some for her. What do you want?" she asked. "Pick anything, and it's on the house."

"Oh no," I began, but then she walked through the double doors without a backward glance, and I was left saying, "That's okay, I'll pay," to myself and the empty room.

A moment later, she returned, presumably with a box of Niki's favorites and approached the glass case. "What'll you have?"

I pointed at a muffin that looked mouthwateringly fattening *and* delicious.

"Chocaholic," Iris said with a smile. "I'll remember that." She used tongs to put a put couple of muffins into the box then taped it closed. "There you go." She passed it over to me, stepping back when I tried to give her some money.

Sighing, I tucked a twenty into the tip jar, ignored her narrowed eyes, then called my goodbyes, walking out the front door.

A few minutes later, I was approaching Niki's house and letting myself in.

It was quiet inside, so I put the box on the counter and peeked inside. Chocolate croissants and chocolate muffins. Two chocoholics, I thought. That was fitting.

I snagged a plate, put a croissant on it, and filled another mug with coffee, bringing both upstairs to Niki's office.

She was on the phone now but aware enough that she saw me come in.

I didn't interrupt, just swapped out the empty mug for the fresh one, found a safe place to stash the plate with the croissant, then brushed my knuckles over her cheek before I slipped back out, shutting the door behind me.

The key burned a hole in my pocket after I'd left a note next to the bakery box, one muffin wrapped in a paper towel, and stepped onto the front porch. But Niki was distracted and upstairs, and I couldn't just leave the house unlocked now, could I?

No. I couldn't.

Just like I couldn't safely leave it under the mat.

Any yahoo might walk up and find it.

What if she had an Amazon delivery, and the dude decided to help him or herself to those baked goods?

Niki might commit murder.

So I locked up, pocketed the key again, and headed to my car. That was the safest course of action for everyone, including the neighborhood delivery drivers.

I drove home with a smile on my face, my heart full, and a muffin in my belly.

Because I just couldn't wait.

CHAPTER SIXTEEN

Niki

I FINALLY TOOK A BREATH, my neck and shoulders aching, and realized I wasn't wearing any pants.

Then I remembered that Archer had come in and out several times.

And I hadn't even acknowledged him.

Because one of our tracing programs, one whose source code I'd written in an effort to infiltrate a certain faction of the Russian mob, had been discovered.

It was supposed to be untraceable, so they shouldn't have been able to trace it back to us.

But it wasn't supposed to have been noticed in the first place.

And that hadn't gone well, had it?

I'd spent who knew how many hours trying to stay ahead of whomever was on the other end, trying to extract the program without them discovering my presence. It had been a challenging shell game, hiding out amongst the code, deleting and adding in secrecy.

Until I'd managed to extract the program. Hopefully,

successfully. But I'd strengthened my firewalls and put every and any security procedure in place that I could think of, just in case.

The unfortunate part was that I hadn't been able to get the information KTS had been after. I'd retrieved *some* stuff that was good for them to know, but the big smoking gun that prosecutors could use and/or the locations of their operatives in the U.S. hadn't been retrieved.

And I fucking hated that I hadn't been able to get my part of the job done.

Even though Laila—my contact at the secret semi-sanctioned government agency—hadn't been mad when I'd reached out to her, we'd both been disappointed that we hadn't gotten what we needed to take the bad guys down.

Neither of us liked to fail.

But I hated more that the failure was on my shoulders.

"Shit," I muttered. "And in all of that, I didn't even acknowledge that Archer brought me coffee and a croissant"—I focused on the clock on my computer, saw it was just past four—"almost eight hours ago."

Processing the time meant that I suddenly became aware of several things, all at once. One, I desperately needed to pee. Two, I was really, really thirsty. Three, I could eat a dozen more of those croissants. And four, probably the most important of all these things, was that I needed to call Archer immediately and apologize.

I snatched my cell from my desk, scrolled to his number, and dialed.

It rang once and went to voicemail, causing my heart to sink.

"Fuck," I whispered, moving out of my office and heading to my bathroom to take care of business then to wash my hands and face, to brush my teeth and turn myself into something that resembled a human.

Then I pushed into my closet, changed, and went downstairs.

I'd fuel up, call him again.

And if he didn't pick up, I was grabbing three cans of tiny raviolis, my loaf of white bread from the fridge, and I was making the man the only dinner I knew how.

I saw the bakery box first.

Then I saw the note.

My heart hiccupped in my chest. My fingers trembled when I reached out to touch it, as though the slip of paper was going to disappear upon contact, as though Archer was going to disappear.

Because chocolate croissants and notes. Coffee and homemade dinners. Chocolate chip pancakes and ice cream sundaes.

Though, *I'd* made the last.

So maybe I was contributing to feeding our stomachs, at least a little bit.

With refined sugar and extra calories and artificial dyes. Not the best.

Also . . . meh. It was *something*.

My fingertips touched the scrap of paper, and it didn't disappear; it didn't just puff away into smoke. Instead, it crinkled, and I picked it up, read slowly, the words moving from my eyes to my brain to my heart in one warm slide.

"Archer," I murmured, holding the paper to my chest.

I read it again because I quite literally couldn't stop myself.

Come by whenever you're done, no matter the hour.
But if you're still working at seven, I'm coming over and
hauling you away from that godforsaken machine.
No arguments. You must listen to the man you're dating (some
might say your boyfriend).
-A
P.S. My guest spot is number twenty-six.

I laughed out loud at the last, even as my emotions swept up and jerked through me like rapids, threatening to pull me under, pushing me this way and that. Until suddenly I was on the other side. The water was still, and so were my emotions. Because . . .

Boyfriend.

Boyfriend.

That should be terrifying.

But instead it was . . . comforting, and also something I wanted so fucking much. If I wasn't living small. If I was pushing outward, an explosion spreading over the earth, expanding until I encompassed everything I'd ever hoped for.

I could do that.

I could go after what I wanted, what I needed. I could have something good, someone who loved me for me.

I could have a man who didn't care that I'd ignored him for work.

Who was thoughtful and didn't care if I fit into a perfect, orderly box.

I could . . .

Get the hell out of my head, leave the baggage firmly behind, and live a giant, no-holds-barred life.

But first—

I ran upstairs, tucked the note carefully in the locked drawer of my desk. Then I headed to the garage, got into my car, and I drove to Archer's apartment.

———

I'D PARKED in spot twenty-six.

I'd knocked.

I'd waited.

I'd called.

And waited some more.

But he didn't answer my call or come to the door, and . . . frankly, I was starting to feel more than a little insecure. He'd left the note. He'd said to come. He'd—

"Enough, Dom—*Niki*," I corrected. "He probably got pulled away to something. You're reading too much into this."

Except, the spot next to twenty-six was his spot.

And his car was there. And he wasn't picking up his phone.

My stomach decided to take up hurdles in my torso, a rise-fall ending with a heavy impact, over and over again. Because . . . what if something had happened and he was hurt or ill inside?

What if—

"Fuck this," I murmured, going back to my car and getting in.

Not because I was going home, but instead because I was retrieving my lockpicks from my center console. Before I'd focused in on unearthing important data, I'd been with a security company, and they'd taught all their techs several useful skills—how to pick a lock, how to avoid getting your face on security cameras, and how to lose a tail.

I'd never had a need to use any of them.

Until today.

Though, I couldn't lie and say that I hadn't been itching to pull out my expertise. I just had hoped it would be under far more exciting and far less nerve-wracking circumstances.

Regardless of nerves and itching, I made my way back up the steps and paused outside Archer's door.

Just to do my due diligence, I knocked again, I called once more.

When neither received a response, I opened the small leather bifold and pulled out the tension wrench and a feeler pick. Then I crouched in front of the door handle, inserted them into the lock, and got to work.

"Whatcha doing?"

I shrieked, dropped the tools where they clanged loudly off the concrete floor, and straightened, covering them with my shoe as I turned to face the man in the hallway. "Nothing," I said, tucking my hands behind me in an effort to shove the rest of my kit into my pocket.

He crossed his arms, a smirk on his face. "Didn't look like nothing."

"I—"

Normally, I might have been able to withstand the man's penetrating expression, to put on some front that sent him screaming and running away, so I could get back to lockpicking my way into Archer's apartment.

Instead, I was truly worried about my boyfriend.

Which was the only reason I could think of for me giving up any pretense and asking, "Do you know Archer? He asked me to come by, and now he's not answering the door or his phone, and I'm worried he might be hurt or sick inside." The man started to shake his head, brows pulling down to frame hazel eyes. "Well, do you have the landlord's number? I think someone should have a spare key to go in, just in case. Just to make sure he's okay—"

The man shook his head again. "I don't have the landlord's number."

Frustration coursed through me, and I bent to pick up my tools, not bothering to hide my intention now. "Fine," I said. "Then I'm going in, and I'm going to make sure he's okay, and if you have a problem with that, you can just try and stop me."

The man waved a hand. "I wouldn't dream of it."

I narrowed my eyes, something familiar about his tone or the words or maybe his face, but I couldn't spend too much time on that.

Not when Archer may be bleeding out on the floor inside.

I inserted the tension wrench, went to work with my pick, flicking the pins into proper alignment with quick *clicks*, and then I was in, pushing the door open and stepping inside. "Feel free to call the cops if you must," I said, when I noticed that the man was recording me with his cell. "Or to trail me inside. I'm not here to steal anything. I just want to—"

"Do some breaking and entering?" he asked.

I sighed, shook my head, and pocketed my tools. "I'm not

—" And then I cut myself off, because the whole bleeding on the floor thing might be happening, and I had more important things to do than try to explain things to a stranger. When I saved Archer's life, he could explain.

The kitchen was empty, as was the bedroom and bathroom.

Which left only one place.

The studio.

I pushed open the door, was momentarily blindsided by a gorgeous landscape of sea green and deep aquamarine before I realized that the studio, too, was empty.

"Find anything?" the man from the hall asked, leaning against the door.

I spun in a circle. "He's not here," I whispered.

That smirk widened. "Apparently not."

"I—"

He held up his cell. "Should I call the police, now? Or did you want to steal something first—"

"Lucas?" Archer called. "Where are you?"

Relief poured through me. He wasn't hurt or bleeding somewhere. He just hadn't . . . picked up my calls? Okay, that didn't feel so great. I opened my mouth to call out to him, but Lucas, apparently, lifted a hand, shook his head.

"Hey fuck head!" Archer called. "You made me carry these bags all the way home without helping, so the least you can do is come out here and put them away."

I blinked.

Lucas just shook his head again.

Archer's voice came closer. "Where are—What the fuck are you doing in my studi . . . *oh?*"

My heart did a tiny somersault, thrusting itself against my rib cage.

No bruises or obvious injuries. No blood or gore.

Just two full arms of groceries.

"Niki?" he said.

I nodded.

"You know her?" Lucas asked, and when Archer nodded, added, "Then you should probably know that she was breaking into your apartment, and I caught her."

Archer's gaze came to mine, some emotion in the hazel depths that I couldn't decipher. Was it disappointment? Disgust that I'd violated his space by breaking in? All my security skills didn't seem quite so *useful* now. "But you didn't actually stop the would-be burglar," he said dryly, his eyes never leaving mine.

"Well, I didn't actually know for certain that she *was* a burglar." A shrug. "So, I decided to keep an eye on her, just in case."

Archer sighed, held my stare for another heartbeat before turning away.

He disappeared.

I'd be lying if I said my stomach didn't return for another round on that roller coaster, looping this way and that, swooping and dipping, and generally making me nauseated.

My fingers clenched around the lockpicks; that sick feeling made its way from my stomach, up my throat, burning as it traveled. "I—"

One more shake of Lucas's head.

And . . .

I lost it.

Who the fuck was this man to shake his head at me, to lift his hand, and to just expect me to fall silent? Fuck that!

I'd given him too much power over me because I was disoriented, standing on a shifting dune of sand, slipping this way and that as I waited to get a handle on the situation.

Well, I needed to *stop* waiting.

I needed . . . I took a step forward, and the cocky bastard started to raise his hand again, and . . .

I snapped.

With a sharp sigh, I shoved the tools in my pocket and

pushed past him, knocking him back a pace when he moved to intercept me.

One hand grabbed my arm, his other snagged the lock-picking paraphernalia out of my pocket. "Wait—"

"Let go," I growled, yanking out of his grip, snagging the tools back. I whirled forward and . . . plowing straight into Archer's chest. "*Oof!*"

Warm arms wrapped around me, steadied me at the same time I was pressed to all the yummy strength of his body, his scent covering me like a blanket, making me feel like I was home. For one brief second.

Because.

Then I remembered the look on his face.

"You said to come over, so I did. And then I called and knocked," I explained. "But nobody answered—"

"That tends to happen when someone isn't home," Lucas pointed out.

"Shut up," Archer barked.

"So then I was there, outside the door, after I'd called and knocked, and I got worried that something had happened, and you were inside hurt." I bit my lip. "So, I called and knocked again. And then . . ."

"You decided to break in," Lucas said.

"I *said*, shut up," Archer gritted, his arms tightening around me for a moment before he slowly drew me away from his chest, wincing when the lockpicking tools jabbed him in the chest. Pausing, he snagged them from my limp fingers and slipped them into his pocket. Then he drew me close again. I didn't want to go, feeling strangely vulnerable, wanting to hide against him forever, lest he see too much. That he'd *see* what I felt for him eclipsed anything I'd ever felt for anyone.

As in, *ever.*

Archer's palm came to my cheek, the rough callouses the sweetest abrasion. "You were worried."

I swallowed. Hard. Nodded.

"So, you broke in?"

Another swallow. Another nod.

Emotion in his eyes, and then his arms banded tightly around me again. "Fuck, Niki. You're killing me," he whispered. "I was just hoping to convince you to let me take care of you, to coax you into spending as much time with me as physically possible." His arms got a little tighter. "I didn't think you'd . . . well, I hoped, but I thought it would take time for you to want to take care of me back."

"You're not mad I broke in?"

He leaned back again. His lips curved. "God no. I'll give you a spare key," he said. "Come and go whenever you want."

My lungs stuttered, breath sliding in and out.

"Okay?" he asked.

I bit my lip, released it. "Okay," I murmured. "I can give you one, too." My mouth turned up. "I know that I can get distracted while I work."

He grinned, ran his knuckles over my cheek. "I noticed that."

A flash of something . . . of guilt? Through his eyes. "What?" I asked.

Archer shifted, reaching into his pocket and pulling out . . . my spare key. "I borrowed this." He shrugged, his expression going chagrined. "I was going to return it . . . okay, no, I was going to hold on to it." He smiled. "I figured if you got mad, I'd just bribe you with food, and—"

Laughter bubbled up inside me, and I closed his fingers around the key. "Keep it."

"Really?"

"Really."

His smile stole my breath, and I didn't get it back because then his mouth was slanting across mine, his tongue slipping inside, his body against me, his arms wrapped tight, and I lost myself in the kiss, in the scent of him.

At least until there was a loud noise breaking in on my bliss.

A throat clearing.

Archer released me with a curse, tucked me against his side, and turned to glare at Lucas.

"I think it's time for you to introduce me to the woman you're sucking face with," he said, his hazel eyes dancing.

Hazel eyes.

Hazel eyes.

Fucking hell. If my arms weren't pinned against Archer's body, I would have reached up and smacked myself across the forehead.

Lucas wasn't familiar because I had seen him before.

"Your Archer's brother!" I exclaimed, feeling like a dolt that it took me that long to recognize that fact.

Lucas smiled, tapped his fingers to his brow in a salute. "One and the same." He smirked. "How many good things has he told you about me?"

I paused, amused despite myself. "A lot actually."

Lucas's smile grew.

"She means nothing," Archer muttered. "I told her you were a pain in my ass, who never knows when to shut up. Especially, when he's a pain in the ass who just shows up out of the blue without any warning."

"Had to check up on my big bro."

Archer rolled his eyes then tugged me toward him as he towed us toward the kitchen. "Hungry?" he asked, coaxing me into a chair as he began going through the bags. "I got stuff to make Bolognese."

"He's already made the pasta dough," Lucas said, sliding into the stool next to me. "I helped."

"By helping, he means by generally being annoying."

Lucas buffed his knuckles on his shoulder. "That's my expertise." He dodged when Archer threw an orange at his head, the fruit bouncing off the wall behind him with a *thunk*, rattling the paintings I'd admired the first time I'd come here.

"Come over here and help me put the groceries away,"

Archer said, and I started to push myself off the seat, but he pointed a finger in my direction. "Not you," he grumbled. "*You*," he said, narrowing his eyes at Lucas. "You're not a guest, so get your ass up off that stool."

"I—"

Archer rounded the island, bent over me and slanted his mouth across mine, his kiss hot and intense and . . . tragically brief.

Because he released me, grabbed his brother's shirt sleeve and brought them both to the other side of the counter. "Groceries," he ordered and turned to the stove.

"I'm only going along with your orders because you're feeding me," Lucas muttered.

I snorted.

Lucas glanced up at me, brows raised.

"It's only, I've said a similar thing to him."

Lucas's lips twitched, and then he laughed. I joined in, cackling when Archer glared at us both before releasing a long-suffering sigh. "Why do I already regret the two of you meeting?"

"Because we're going to team up?" I asked.

Lucas reached across the island and held up his hand for me to high five.

Archer sighed again.

My lips curved.

His did, too.

And I knew this was going to be one of the best nights of my life.

CHAPTER SEVENTEEN

Archer

I'D SLIPPED a key into her purse before dinner was even finished cooking.

Not that I worried I'd forget, but rather that I couldn't help myself. I wanted to have that link with her.

So when she went off to use the bathroom, I'd tucked it safely onto her key chain, along with returning her lockpicking tools—a story I'd need to get all the details to at a later point.

Later, because Lucas had shown up out of the blue a couple of hours before, a duffle bag in one hand, a carefree smile on his lips, and totally and effortlessly interrupting my plans with Niki. Then he'd abandoned me in the grocery store, leaving me to carry the food home, food he'd mostly selected because he had terrible eating habits and my normal healthy fare wouldn't satisfy his taste buds.

Not that I wasn't happy to see my brother.

It was just . . . I had plans.

With Niki.

Plans without a third wheel of my annoying, awesome, frustrating, exceptional younger brother, who'd charmed Niki far more easily than I had been able to. A fact I like to consider was because she wasn't attracted to him—because she'd liked me too much to let me get close so quickly, right?—either that or she just liked Lucas better.

Rolling my eyes at myself, I gathered the sleeping Niki closer.

She was cuddled against my chest, having succumbed to sleep before the first episode of the show we'd put on after dinner had finished.

My chest.

So, she clearly liked me better.

I allowed myself one more eye roll and then ran my fingers through her hair as I turned my gaze back to the TV.

Lucas's voice was soft, barely reaching my ears. He reached for the remote, paused the show. "I like her, Arch."

My heart squeezed. "Me, too."

"She's different."

"Yes," I agreed, running my hand lightly up and down her back. She was different, a juxtaposition of fearful and brave, of smart and capable, of beautiful and fragile. But strong. She was mostly strong, because she'd managed to put that fear aside and give me a shot.

I wasn't going to fuck it up.

"She's *really* different," he said.

"Yes," I agreed again.

"You should marry her."

I froze, my arms seizing so tightly that she frowned against my chest. Quickly, I released her, ran my hand up and down her back again, settling her, waiting until her face relaxed again before acknowledging Lucas's statement. "I just got her to agree to date me," I said. "It would be a stretch to get her to accept a proposal."

My brother smirked. "You are difficult to stomach."

I chucked a pillow in his direction, but because I didn't want to jostle Niki too much and risk waking her, I missed by a mile.

"Getting old enough that your eyesight is going?"

"Fuck off."

"I will," he said. "Tomorrow, because I don't want to drive home through the night."

My heart had been doing all sorts of squeezing over the last few days, but it didn't appear that the reaction would be stopping any time soon. "Luc?" I asked.

Wary hazel eyes coming to mine. "Yeah?"

"Thanks." I swallowed, my throat suddenly tight. "For everything you did. I—I—" I inhaled, exhaled slowly. "I wouldn't have gotten through it without you."

Lucas's expression went serious for once. "You would have." I wasn't sure I believed that. "And, before you start rejecting that idea, just think about all the times you were there and saved my ass. I'm not even talking about how I wouldn't have gotten through identifying their bodies, their funerals, and taking care of everything with their estate. I'm talking about being a pain in the ass kid with a chip on his shoulder who liked to stir up shit." The corner of his mouth quirked up. "I would have gotten my ass beaten way more times than actually happened if you hadn't had my back."

Read: we'd both gotten our asses kicked a shit-ton until I'd figured out how to fight back then had taught Luc.

Good times.

Also, the best times. Everything was so much simpler then— stupid kids doing stupid shit, stealing our parents' booze, hiding out in the field behind our house getting drunk (being stupid), smoking pot, and bringing whatever group of friends and girls we'd managed to convince to hang out with us.

Mostly because we'd had alcohol.

Also because my brother was funny as hell.

But at the foundation of all of that had always been Lucas and me. The two of us, and I wouldn't give up that time for anything.

"So what I'm saying" —Luc's voice was a little hoarse, the emotion in his voice making my eyes burn— "is that I will always be there for you." He cleared his throat, the mischief returning. "Even if it's just playing best man at another wedding."

I sighed. "We've been over this," I said. "I just got divorced."

My brother smirked and reclined on the couch. "Just saying, if I were you and in love with a woman like Niki, I'd lock it in as soon as possible."

Love.

In love.

My heart thudded in my chest, my fingers convulsed, sinking into Niki's soft curves as that thought flowed over me, as I poked and prodded it, just for good measure. Did I love her?

How . . . could I not?

I let the truth flow over me, settle over my brain like a warm blanket, comfort sinking into me as reality struck home.

I loved her.

Of course I did.

"You're a pain in my ass," I grumbled.

"And damned proud of it."

I tossed another pillow, my aim this time true.

It flew through the air and . . . smacked him right across the face.

"Hey!" he muttered, snatching it and winding up like he was going to throw it back. Then his eyes narrowed. "You're lucky I don't want to hit Niki."

"I love you, too, Luc," I said.

Those eyes stayed narrowed. Then he stuck the pillow behind his head and curled his legs underneath him. "Shut up so we can watch the show."

I shut up.

He hit play on the show.

And just as it began rolling again, my brother said, "I love you, too."

My heart did some more of that somersaulting.

Because, damn, the fucker was good.

CHAPTER EIGHTEEN

Niki

I HEARD the door *click* closed downstairs and hurried to finish my email.

I'd just met with a new client, and I like to summarize the tasks contracted, especially when I had a feeling said client would be a pain in the ass.

Contrary to any pseudo-legal researching like I did with KTS, this client was fully legitimate—although maybe legitimate wasn't the right term because KTS was a real patron of mine, and they paid in real money. It was just that the organization didn't always operate under strictly legal means, even though several governments had sanctioned the project.

So anyway, this research would be less hacking and more actual research. Although, I would get to place a tracing program, and hopefully I'd worked out any kinks that had enabled it to be detected before.

The research, however, *would* be secret. The email going to an untraceable inbox that only the CEO and I could access.

The Fortune 500 company had contracted me after having received a tip that the CFO was embezzling. It was my job to track down the proof of that, to deliver it to the CEO and only the CEO. They'd handle the CFO in whatever way they handled him, although—and I'd made this very clear—if I found that innocent people's money or assets were affected in any way and the company didn't make that right, then *I* would make it right.

And they wouldn't like my solution.

Smiling, I finished the email and hit send, shutting everything down before I left my office, stopping in the hall to check that I had indeed put on pants that morning. (For the record, I had). Then I made my way into the kitchen to find Archer putting groceries away.

It had been a month since I'd met Lucas, and we'd fallen into a routine. The nights he wasn't working, he came here and cooked dinner. The nights he was, and if I didn't need to stay glued to my computer all evening, I went to the bar and stuffed myself full of yummy, fried food.

So basically, I was eating better than I ever had in my life.

Though, I did occasionally sneak a can of tiny ravioli if I managed to surface from work at lunchtime.

Also, I was going to have to buy new jeans if I continued this way, either that or go pants-less, and I found that I didn't care because . . . Archer had unpacked the grocery bags and pulled out ingredients for . . . *Bolognese!*

"Bolognese! Bolognese!" I said, doing a little happy dance, which had him glancing up and smiling then hooking his arm around my waist and drawing me close.

"How was your day?" he asked, nuzzling my throat.

"Mmm," was the only response I could muster, especially when his hands began to wander, slipping down to cup my ass then drifting up to brush the outsides of my breasts.

I wanted them to touch the insides.

I *wanted* them on my bare skin.

Which was why I pushed him back, reached for the hem of my shirt and tugged it over my head.

"But what about the Bolognese?" he asked, his fingers gripping the bottom of his tee, yanking it up and over his head. "I know how hungry you get."

I was hungry all right. For his cock. For rough, warm hands on bare skin. For his mouth on mine, on my nipples, my pussy. It had been almost twenty-four hours since I'd had him, and I wanted him like it was the first time every time. Need that wove through me, making my hands tremble, my thighs clench, that had me walking over to him and flicking open the button on his jeans.

The zzz of his zipper sliding down was the best sound ever.

"Not hungry," he murmured, brushing my hands away. His jeans were precariously perched, open and loose, hanging on the edges of his hips, and the temptation to nudge it down, to slip my hand into his boxer briefs, to enjoy the treasure within —*ha, but also true*—was intense. Whether he read that in my eyes or was just experiencing temptation of his own, I didn't know. All I *did* know was that one second, I was staring at the hard ridge of his cock, imagining how delicious it would be to lick it like my favorite lollipop, and the next, my pants were on the ground, my ass on the edge of the counter.

"Magician," I teased.

"My next trick," he said, leaning close and kissing a spot beneath my jaw, "is to make your bra disappear." And then he lent action to words by reaching behind me and flicking open the clasp on my bra.

"Next thing I know," I said, running my fingers over the bristles on his jaw, "you'll be pulling a rabbit out of a hat . . . or maybe a condom out of thin air."

He reached into his pocket. "How about a condom out of denim?" he asked, holding up the plastic square, his lips curved into a sexy smile I just had to kiss. So I did . . . and then I gave in to the urge to push down those pants.

One nudge and they hit the tile.

Another and his boxers joined them.

He set the condom on the counter, pulled back, and brushed

his thumb over my bottom lip, trailed it down my throat, across my chest, massaging one breast then the other, rolling my nipples between thumb and forefinger. Oh fuck, that was good. I jerked, pleasure flowing through me, damp heat pooling between my thighs. "You're a magician now, too?"

"Hmm?"

"You made my pants disappear," he said, bending to take one aching tip into his mouth, suckling deeply.

My fingers found his hair, clenched tight, but he wasn't deterred. Instead, he continued using his mouth and hands to whip my need into a frenzied froth of desire, lungs burning, pussy drenched and aching in emptiness, my lips and fingers tingling.

I snagged the condom from the counter, tore it open with my teeth, and rolled it down the length of his cock.

His forehead dropped to my shoulder, hot breath puffing on skin, fingers drifting down, slipping between my slick heat, one circled the bud of nerves, sending wave after wave of bliss through me.

"Enough," I said, pushing his hand away and reaching for his cock, gripping it tight and tugging it toward me.

And then he was inside, the crown of him stretching me tight, filling me full to the brim as he pressed deep in slow, incremental strokes, bottoming out, coaxing my legs around his waist. "Closer, baby," he murmured, tugging me toward the edge of the counter in one quick move that brought him even deeper and had me gasping, gripping the square lip.

"Sorry," he murmured.

"I'm not," I said, wrapping my legs tighter, using my heels to encourage him to grind against me.

Sparks of pleasure flew through me, gathering together into a thick rope that wound through my insides, stiffening my spine, a tiny ball of fire, of pleasure growing in my abdomen, expanding until it filled every part of me, licking over my nerves, tightening my muscles, until . . .

Boom.

Explosion.

In cinders.

My head fell back as he continued moving, sparking the embers into an orgasm that went on and on and *on*.

He groaned, hips jerking, my name tumbling from his lips as he found his own climax, and then we were both wrapped in pleasure, both soaring together, both slowly, oh so slowly, coming back down to earth.

We stayed in place for long minutes, but eventually reality intruded, the cold and hard of the counter seeping into my ass, the cool air prickling along my skin.

I kept my arms and legs wrapped tight around him, not ready to let go.

My heartbeat slowed. The sweat evaporated on my skin . . .

My stomach growled.

Loudly.

Archer laughed, his arms tightening around me, the warm puffs of his chuckles on my throat. He leaned back, cupped my cheek. "Bolognese."

CHAPTER NINETEEN

Archer

I POKED my head through the door, saw Niki typing away, and started to turn and go back downstairs, but she spun in her chair.

"Wait," she said, extending a hand in my direction. "I just need to finish this email"—she turned back to her computer, pressed a few final keys, and clicked her mouse—"and . . . *done!*" She smiled, ran her hand through her hair in a motion I'd seen often enough to understand it was one of those small, unconscious movements that one only learned about their partner when they'd spent enough time together.

And we'd spent a lot of time together.

Every free moment outside of work.

Laughing together in front of the TV, cuddling in bed talking about nothing at all. Her glaring at me from across the bar, smiling when I snuck a Sex on the Beach in front of her—or as we'd begun calling it, Sex on the Seats, since she'd said my ability to mix vodka, juice, and schnapps had gotten me a free ride right into her pants.

But more than the sex and the eating—both of which were great—I found that Niki was a friend.

A good friend.

My best friend.

I'd never found someone who was so easy to be with. From the moment she'd decided to let me in, to date me, our relationship had been effortless in a way it had *never* been with my ex.

Right.

This with Niki was right. I was head over heels in love with her, I'd fallen hard and deep and fast, and I knew it was the absolute best thing I'd ever had in my life. The only thing that would make it better—literally, the *only* thing—would be if my parents were around to meet her.

They would love her just as intensely.

And Niki deserved to have parents like I'd had.

Unfortunately, I couldn't resurrect the dead or change people who were despicable. I could, however, love Niki, and we could build our family around us.

Family that was coming over to her house for dinner.

She pushed to her feet, crossed to me, coming into my arms with a pinched expression that had her winged brows drawing into a V.

I brushed my finger over them, smoothing the frown away. "What is it?"

"I'm nervous," she said, wrinkling her nose in a way that had me aching to tumble her onto the bed and make love to her until she forgot all about being worried. "How stupid is that? It's not like I need to impress them." She did that thing with her hair again. "Did you know I took a break this morning and scrubbed the grout in the bathroom with a toothbrush?"

I guided her toward the stairs. "I, for one, approve."

She made a sound of disgust. "It was already clean. I did my whirlwind of *that* yesterday. I don't think this place has been so neat and organized and *scrubbed* since I moved in."

"I, for one—*oof!*" I said, busting into laughter when she smacked me.

"You're not funny."

"Except, I *am.*"

A huff. "Archer," she warned.

"It'll be fine," I said. "Your place needed the cleaning, though"—I kissed the tip of her nose as we reached the first floor—"I told you, I'd help you with that."

"It's my place—"

"My mess," I said, finishing the statement she said every time she caught me cleaning something in her place. "Again." I cupped both of her cheeks, tilted her head up so I could slant my lips over hers. "But I don't mind helping the woman I love," I murmured. "In fact, I enjoy it because it means that I take something off her plate when she's already managing a lot."

She'd finished a big corporate job the week before and then had been roped into a government assignment she couldn't talk to me about. All I knew was that it had meant she hardly left her office for close to three days.

Then she'd had a breakthrough and things had calmed down a bit and—

My thoughts trailed to a halt when I caught a glimpse of the expression on her face, the stiffness in her body.

"What is it?" I asked.

Her lips parted, pressed flat. Parted again.

I mentally backtracked through what I'd said.

Working a lot. Not minding helping her. The woman . . . *I loved.*

Oh, fucking hell. I hadn't meant to say it like that. I'd had a whole plan to introduce it slowly, to get her used to the idea of how well we work together, how good we were as a couple. And *then* I'd planned to tell her.

Maybe while she was handcuffed to my headboard, so she couldn't escape.

I certainly hadn't meant to say it aloud.

Especially when it turned her into Statue Niki.

"I . . . um . . ." I wasn't going to take it back. I couldn't, not when it was the truth. "Are you okay?"

Still, she played a statue.

"Niki."

She inhaled, but her eyes were still far away, her face pale, and she was trembling.

"Baby?" I asked.

Continuing to breathe, but still not out of the fog, her every muscle taut and rigid.

"Are you okay?" I whispered, smoothing my hand over her hair.

She didn't unstick, exactly, but a sound emerged from her throat, at least. "I—"

Fuck. I'd broken her. Surprised her and reset her brain, and now I needed to find a way to melt the ice in her veins to make the panic she was certainly feeling subside, so I could go back to winning her over in increments. I rested my hand on her shoulder, slid it in, and stroked my thumb up and down her throat. She was still tense, but she hadn't bustled me out the front door, hadn't run upstairs and locked herself into her office. So, that was something. But how to snap her out of this, to get her to push through the fog? What could I possibly say to—

"Bolognese?" I blurted.

She blinked, head jerking, eyes widening. "What?" she whispered.

Apparently, now I was finally speaking her love language. "Bolognese," I said again.

Her mouth opened, a breath sliding out. "What are you talking about?"

"Nothing," I said. "I . . ." I sighed. "Are you okay?"

She blinked, shoulders rising and falling on a breath, confusion being replaced by uncertainty. "Did you mean it?"

I inhaled sharply.

"Because if you didn't—"

The doorbell rang.

"Niki—"

She spun toward the front hall, hurrying away from me as though it were her job and she was going to get the best employee evaluation ever, twisting the handle and opening it before I had the chance to say anything further.

Kace and Brooke, Iris and Brent, Hayden and Anabelle all poured into the house, their arms full of bags and bottles.

It was the first time they'd all taken the night off, leaving the bar in the hands of Bobby's other employees, and for Kace, taking a much-needed Friday off.

"Sorry we're late," Iris said, passing Niki a bakery box before giving her a one-armed hug, "I had to pry Brooke off her computer."

"I was in the middle of a scene!" Brooke complained, hugging Niki as soon as Iris released her.

"As much as I love your books, Archer promised to cook for us." She pointed at her belly, curved gently with new life inside. "There's a baby in here who needs some of the food that Niki keeps tormenting us about."

Niki, for one, appeared shell-shocked.

Whether that was from the sudden noise and conversation or my slip of the tongue—or both—I couldn't be sure. Either way, she was still a statue, although a living, breathing one.

So maybe some animatronic robot or—

Maybe this wasn't important because Niki was clearly terrified and overwhelmed, and I needed to do something to put my best friend and the woman I loved at ease.

And deal with the crowd of people in the hall.

Hayden, Niki's righthand man, glanced from his boss to me to the crowd and said, "Hey, I had a quick question about—"

"No shop-talk!" Iris protested.

But Hayden was skilled at maneuvering, and so was I. Sometimes, anyway. When it didn't come to declarations of love, that was.

Or botched ones.

Or any variety, I supposed.

Regardless, work would give Niki a cushion, a moment to come out of her shock, and then I could corral our friends, put them to work cutting noodles. Then I'd take my woman aside, would tell her in no uncertain terms that I most certainly loved her, and I didn't give a fuck if that notion scared her, because I wasn't like her parents or her former fiancé. I wasn't just going to leave. I loved every part of her, and I was staying around.

Okay?

Okay then.

Hayden met my eyes and lifted his chin in the direction of the kitchen. I nodded gratefully, shepherded the rest of the flock away, thanking the universe that Hayden was able to read his boss.

Ten minutes later, I'd gotten the girls to roll up their sleeves, Iris supervising as Anabelle and Brooke rolled out the pasta dough I'd premade and then cut the fettuccini noodles, Kace reheating the sauce on the stovetop. Bread was covered, courtesy of Iris and her bakery, along with wine and salad, the two which both, surprisingly, were from the bar.

Not the wine, I supposed.

That made sense.

But the salad.

It was fresh and delicious and the second bestseller behind the sampler basket of fried goodness. Local produce made that easy, along with a large subset of their customers who liked to "pretend" to be healthy by ordering a salad to go along with all that bar food.

"Pretend" because that's what a few of their regulars— Abby, Bec, Sera, CeCe, and Rachel—called it when they came in for their weekly dinner date. Sometimes with husbands. Sometimes with kids. *Always* with lots of laughter and affection.

Their regulars were the best.

That aside, I had the food part of the evening covered.

Everyone's belly would get filled, wine would be drunk, and good times would be had, even by Niki. I'd make that happen. I'd give my left nut to make that happen.

But as time passed, my eyes drifting to the doorway, neither Hayden nor Niki making an appearance, I started to get tetchy.

She was probably in panic mode, and the distraction at work had just been temporary and—

Breathe.

It would be okay.

I'd talk to her and all would be okay.

I set the table, opened and poured the wine . . . and kept checking for Niki.

After fifteen minutes, I heard footsteps and relaxed when Hayden walked into the kitchen. But that tension returned almost immediately because Niki didn't follow.

Hayden came and got two glasses of wine from me. "She's okay. Just in the bathroom."

I nodded but didn't feel reassured as he moved off to bring the wine to Anabelle. In fact, I was so on edge, every cell in my body telling me that I needed to find Niki and speak to her immediately, that I'd actually taken a step back when Iris called out for my help.

"I'm a baker not a pasta maker, Archer," she said. "What do we do now?"

My gaze was on the opening, hoping that Niki would . . . just . . . come . . . *in.*

"Just put them in the water," I said.

"Um . . ."

Something about Iris's tone had me turning back . . . and immediately wincing at the mess that had become of my pasta dough.

My brows lifted.

Iris plunked her hands on her hips. "I said I was a baker, not a pasta maker."

That, I could see.

"I am neither a baker nor a pasta maker," Anabelle said, a chunk of dough in her hair.

"Me, too," Brooke said, her entire front covered in flour. "I can *write* a book about making pasta, but I can't roll it out for shit."

That, also, I could see.

Sighing, I tore my gaze from the opening, put down the bottle, and headed over to rescue dinner from the hands of the trio. I'd give Niki a few more minutes before busting down the door to the bathroom.

"Okay," I said, "non-bakers and pasta makers, *this* is how you roll out dough."

CHAPTER TWENTY

Niki

AFTER ARCHER'S *woman I love* slipup (Was it a slipup? Was it real? Did I want it to be real? Was I fucking terrified to want that?) I seriously considered running out the front door.

But there were two problems with that.

One, it was my house.

Where would I run to? I supposed I could buy another house, in a city far away from any and all men named Archer who said insane things like *I love*, but I wouldn't be able to sneak my computer equipment out without him seeing, and I needed my equipment so I could work and pay for the new house, and I couldn't just go out and buy a new computer because I'd built my current setup. So no, I was too attached to my beauty of a system to just replace it with something *store-bought*.

Two, my other problem with just running, was . . . well, I didn't want to run.

I liked being with Archer.

It was easy and beautiful, and I couldn't picture going back to my life how it had been before.

How could I give him up?

And yet, how could I keep him? Wouldn't love bring complications and more emotions and more ways for me to let him down?

I couldn't love him. *I couldn't.*

It was just better to be boyfriend and girlfriend, extreme like on both sides, nothing complicated like love. Then we'd stay lovers, stay friends, stay together, and I wouldn't have to give him up.

Yes, I was ignoring the fact that most boyfriends and girl-friends moved toward love and that many moved toward—swallowing hard—marriage.

Yes, I was also ignoring the fact that I was a coward.

Because when he'd said *woman I love,* my heart had squeezed hard, joy had bubbled through my veins like sparkling water, and longing had gripped every single part of me.

I wanted that.

But how?

When I just had the huge boulder sitting on my chest, telling me that I couldn't do this, revisiting all the doubts I'd clung to for so long.

So cowardice and longing and feeling like the woman I'd been several months before.

Fucking hell.

Which was why I'd run upstairs under the guise of going to the bathroom after talking about nothing important with regards to work with Hayden. He was too observant by half, and I knew he'd been trying to give me a second to breathe and refocus by thinking about the one thing that always centered me —work.

But how could I?

Because it suddenly wasn't the most important thing in my life.

Which was why I was in my office, trying not to hyperventilate while my friends, while the family I'd begun forming, were gathered downstairs, their laughter and conversation flowing up through the floor.

Sighing, but no closer to courage, I forced myself to leave my sanctuary and move into the bedroom.

Baby steps.

I'd just tell Archer to cool it on the whole love thing, that we just needed to keep dating and that was it, none of the pesky L-word to muck things up. We'd just keep things exactly like they were, and they'd stay great, and it would be perfect.

And I wouldn't ruin it.

I wouldn't—

Gaze drifting to the bed, to the bare wall above it, I nearly tripped over my own two feet. Perhaps, formerly bare was more appropriate.

No, there wasn't anything *perhaps* about it.

It was occupied.

With a huge, colorful painting of . . .

Us.

It was abstract, the shapes and lines blurred together into something that wouldn't be immediately recognizable, but it also *was* instantly identifiable because I was part of it. Because it was Archer *with* me.

I could picture the moment—him smiling down at me, his arms wrapped tight, his face so close that I could feel the heat of his breath, the individual bristles of his beard, see the tiny scar just above his right eyebrow.

Us.

My feet carried me to the bed, on top of it, my fingers tracing over the strokes of paint, and I *knew.*

This was fear talking.

This was fear trying to pull me back down, to shrink my life into that tiny, miserable bubble.

But I'd slipped an arm and a leg out of it and it was *good.*

No. It was fantastic.

Because the feelings that Archer, that our relationship invoked weren't small and contained, they weren't something I could just mess up and ruin. They were deep and important and not something that shoved me down, tied me up.

And as I stood there, staring at the painting, I realized they weren't something to be feared.

He loved me.

Me.

Not some version of myself I tried and failed to be for my parents.

Not the me, who'd tried to lash out and keep people at a distance.

Just the me who was . . . myself.

The workaholic, messy and unorganized, tiny ravioli eating *me.*

Heart pounding, one second my fingers were running along the rough canvas and the next, they were trailing through the air as I ran out of my bedroom, down the stairs, and into the kitchen.

My heart pounded. My chest heaved.

But not from the exertion.

Rather, it was from the realization. From the sudden focus of seven people on me. From the one person who mattered the most.

Archer.

Who was straining the pot of pasta, steam filling the space between him and the pot, the air filled with the scent of Bolognese, with the sound of teasing and joy, and I burst out from that small box.

Firmly and forever.

"I love you," I blurted.

The room fell silent.

Clang.

I jumped when the pot slipped out of Archer's hands, but I barely had time to register the noise before he was in front of me, flour on his cheek, his eyes wide, his voice hoarse when he asked, "What did you say?"

"I love you," I repeated, not needing courage. Not now. Not after seeing that painting, after understanding.

He loved *me*.

I watched his neck work, saw his eyes grow damp, his words a bare whisper as he said, "You do?"

I nodded, cupped his jaw, the bristles of his beard a rough caress on my palms. "I do," I whispered back. "How could I not? You see all the things that others find as flaws, and you accept them as something wonderful. You love the pain in the ass, the slob, the woman who sometimes doesn't have the courage to voice the feelings in her heart." I slid my hand down to his chest, feeling *his* heart pounding against his ribs. "So, how could I not love the wonderful man who cooks for me, who cares about me, who tried to make my life easier? Who makes me Bolognese, even though it's a pain in the ass." His lips curved. "Who loves me, just as I am. Not changes requested or insults slung. Just acceptance and patience and"—I chuckled —"sometimes stubborn persistence."

He stroked his knuckles along the back of my throat. "You forgot about vodka."

I covered his hand with mine. "I didn't," I whispered. "I didn't forget *anything* about you, and I never will."

He ran his thumb over my bottom lip. "I feel so damned lucky you sat in that stool."

"And that the ladies at the other end of the bar ordered too many drinks?"

Archer shook his head. "No."

"No?" I asked.

His eyes twinkled. "No, they didn't order too many drinks. I needed a way to talk to you, and I was desperate to get you to unleash the full force of your glare on me."

I burst out laughing. "You're sick."

"No," he said, grasping the side of my neck and hauling me close. "I'm absolutely, totally, completely, endlessly—"

"That's a lot of -lys."

A finger over my lips. "Shh," he said, "I'm trying to be romantic."

More laughter, but this time it was mixed with the type of incandescent joy that only this man wrought.

"Where was I?" He tapped his lips this time. "Intensely, irrevocably . . . foreverly—"

"That's not a word."

"Shh," he said.

"Archer," I warned. "So help me, God, but do I need to threaten your murder via kitchen tools again?"

"You love me," he countered.

"I'm already regretting it."

"I'm not," he said, tugging me close and resting his forehead to mine. "It's the greatest gift you could have ever given me."

I rose on tiptoe. He bent.

And our mouths, like every other part of us—our bodies, our hearts, our souls—lined up perfectly.

"Um," Brooke began. "I don't mean to break up the romantic moment," she said, concern creeping into her voice and at the same time, the smell hit my nose. "But Kace burned the sauce."

"It wasn't on purpose!" he exclaimed, wincing as he glanced down into the pot.

"I don't trust *any* of you when it comes to burning things," Iris said.

Anabelle glanced from the pot, her wince rivaling Kace's. "Got caught up in the romance, did you?"

"Shut it," he grumbled. "This isn't my fault. I should have never been trusted with something as important as Bolognese duty."

Archer's chest vibrated with laughter.

Hayden held up his phone. "I'm ordering dinner from the bar," he said. "Who wants what?"

Orders were called across the room. The ruined sauce—and pasta, since Archer had managed to miss the colander altogether—went into the trash. More wine was poured (and tacked onto the order from the bar).

But teasing abounded, along with love and even more laughter.

Still in Archer's arms, I smiled up at him, at the man I loved, so blissfully happy I could barely breathe.

This moment wasn't perfect.

I wasn't perfect.

Our relationship, our love wouldn't be perfect either.

But it was *perfectly* imperfect for us.

And that was enough.

Hate missing Elise's new releases? Love contests, exclusive excerpts and giveaways?

Then signup for Elise's newsletter here!

http://eepurl.com/bdnmEj

LOVE AFTER MIDNIGHT

Rum And Notes

Virgin Daiquiri

On The Rocks

Sex On The Seats

LOVE AFTER MIDNIGHT

Did you miss any of the Love After Midnight Books? See below for sneak peeks at the series and
check out www.elisefaber.com/love-after-midnight-series for more information!
And don't forget to signup for my newsletter for ALL the release information http://eepurl.com/bdnmEj

———

Rum And Notes
Book 1
www.books2read.com/RumAndNotes

Brooke

"WANT A FRESH ONE?"

My eyes flew up from the glass to meet Kace's.

"Um," I murmured. "Sure. But can you add a little rum?"

A flash of white teeth. "All done, then?" He leaned toward me, resting his forearms on the bar, the long sleeves of his shirt riding up to reveal just the edge of a tattoo. I'd seen the whole tat before. On Day 36. He'd worn short sleeves for a change, a bone thrown to the unseasonably hot weather that day, and suddenly my hero had gotten tattoos, beautiful swirling lines crawling along his skin, sweeping around and up his forearms, twisting together and disappearing under the cotton of his short sleeves, tempting a woman to trace them with her tongue.

No.

My heroine's tongue.

Fantasy was fine, so long as I kept it between the pages.

I bit my bottom lip until the mental image faded, kept my tongue firmly in my mouth, and nodded at Kace.

He rapped his knuckles against the counter once, reciprocated my nod, then snagged my glass and turned away, dumping the contents, adding ice, rum, then soda before coming back over to me. He plunked the drink on the bar, but when I went to reach for it, he rested his hand on mine. "What are you working on so diligently?" he asked, and the contact, paired with his eyes locked on mine, stole my breath.

"Wh-what?"

His response was to release my hand, and while I was mourning the loss of his touch, he grabbed my computer, spun it to face him, and opened it.

"No—"

But it was too late.

It was open, the screen lighting up, illuminating his sharp but beautiful features, and he was reading.

Oh fuck, he was reading!

I made a mad grab for the laptop, but he swept it off the bar, lifting it in the air and continuing to read. My computer obscured most of his face, but not his eyebrows. Those brows kept rising until they were tight sideways C's on his forehead, well above the edge of my screen.

Then he lowered the laptop and stared at me.

"*This* is what you've been writing?"

In fairness, he'd caught me in the middle of a hot scene, made hotter because he'd been my inspiration for it.

A fact he seemed to understand when his eyes met mine. "Jace?"

I coughed. "It's a common name."

"Blue eyes?" He glanced back at the screen. "Tats? Brown hair?"

"Not an uncommon combination." I picked up my glass, drained it, eyes watering against the burn.

"A scar on the right side of his bottom lip?" he asked, putting my laptop down.

Okay, *now* was the time for running.

Something I normally abhorred, but in this case, it was critical. I snatched up my computer, reached into my wallet and pulled out some cash, and tossed it on the bar.

Then I jumped off the stool and ran.

—Rum And Notes (books2read.com/RumAndNotes)

———

Virgin Daiquiri
Book 2
www.books2read.com/VirginDaiquiri

Brent

Fuck. Someone needed to save this woman from herself.

That someone couldn't be me.

But that still didn't stop me from snagging her arm and rotating her to face me. "You live near the city now. You have to be smart." Her lips parted again, probably to tell me she *was* smart, but I kept talking. "*Street* smart. You can't tell strange men you live alone *or* invite them back to your place."

"Fine," she said.

"Fine," I agreed.

But I didn't let her go.

Her eyes flicked over my shoulder, to the ceiling, and my gaze followed hers, half-expecting to see a giant spider dangling there.

Instead, I saw mistletoe.

I glanced back down. She licked her lips.

And suddenly, I knew she was thinking the same thing as me. Warm bodies pressed together, lips only inches apart, heat filling the space, and a kiss-inducing plant overhead.

"Mistletoe," she whispered and licked her lips again.

Just one taste.

I could give myself that.

I bent my head and slanted my mouth across hers.

—Virgin Daiquiri (books2read.com/VirginDaiquiri)

———

On the Rocks

Book 3

www.books2read.com/ontherocksef

Anabelle

"Don't."

I stopped mid-bend at the male voice.

"I've got it."

Tall. *Really* tall. Dark hair with a reddish tint. Olive skin. Bright blue eyes. And, *oh NBD*, maybe also the most handsome man I'd ever met.

I swallowed hard then frowned when he reached past me to close the door.

Then frowned harder when he rang the doorbell.

"Um," I began, wanting to ask him what in the ever-loving-fuck he was doing. But the doorbell had been rung and footsteps approached, and the wooden panel swung back open to reveal Brooke standing on the threshold, smile wide. "Did you forget something, An . . . a . . . *belle?*"

The smile faded from Brooke's face.

Her olive skin went pale.

Her eyes widened. Her eyes . . . that were the same shape as those of the man towering over me on the porch.

Kace came up behind her. "Everything okay—"

Brooke didn't answer him, just reached a hand out as though she expected to encounter a ghost, her voice shaking when she spoke.

"Hayden?"

—On the Rocks—www.books2read.com/ontherocksef

ALSO BY ELISE FABER FABER

Crashed (July 27th, 2021)

Breakers Hockey (all stand alone)

Broken (May 24th, 2021)

KTS Series

Fire and Ice (Hurt Anthology, stand alone)

Riding The Edge

Crossing The Line

Leveling The Field (June 14th, 2021)

Love, Action, Camera (all stand alone)

Dotted Line

Action Shot

Close-Up

End Scene

Meet Cute

Love After Midnight (all stand alone)

Rum And Notes

Virgin Daiquiri

On The Rocks

Sex On The Seats (April 26th, 2021)

Life Sucks Series (all stand alone)

Train Wreck

Hot Mess

Dumpster Fire

Clusterf*@k (August 16th, 2021)

Roosevelt Ranch Series (all stand alone, series complete)

Disaster at Roosevelt Ranch

Heartbreak at Roosevelt Ranch

Collision at Roosevelt Ranch

Regret at Roosevelt Ranch

Desire at Roosevelt Ranch

Phoenix Series (read in order)

Phoenix Rising

Dark Phoenix

Phoenix Freed

Phoenix: LexTal Chronicles (rereleasing soon, stand alone, Phoenix world)

From Ashes

In Flames

To Smoke (October 18th, 2021)

Stand Alones

Someday, Maybe (YA)

ABOUT THE AUTHOR

USA Today bestselling author, Elise Faber, loves chocolate, Star Wars, Harry Potter, and hockey (the order depending on the day and how well her team -- the Sharks! -- are playing). She and her husband also play as much hockey as they can squeeze into their schedules, so much so that their typical date night is spent on the ice. Elise changes her hair color more often than some people change their socks, loves sparkly things, and is the mom to two exuberant boys. She lives in Northern California. Connect with her in her Facebook group, the Fabinators or find more information about her books at www.elisefaber.com.

f facebook.com / elisefaberauthor

a amazon.com / author / elisefaber

BB bookbub.com / profile / elise-faber

O instagram.com / elisefaber

g goodreads.com / elisefaber

P pinterest.com / elisefaberwrite

www.ingramcontent.com/pod-product-compliance
Lightning Source LLC
Chambersburg PA
CBHW031023260626
47153CB00018B/2794